THE HIDDEN PRINCESS

Other books by Katy Moran:

Bloodline
Bloodline Rising
Spirit Hunter
Dangerous to Know
Hidden Among Us

THE HIDDEN PRINCESS

KATY MORAN

WALKER BOOKS

First published in 2014 by Walker Books Ltd
87 Vauxhall Walk, London SE11 5HJ

2 4 6 8 10 9 7 5 3 1

Text © 2014 Katy Moran
Cover illustration © 2014 Alejandro Colucci

The right of Katy Moran to be identified as author of this work has been asserted by her in accordance with the Copyright, Designs and Patents Act 1988

This book has been typeset in Bembo

Printed and bound in Great Britain by Clays Ltd, St Ives plc

British Library Cataloguing in Publication Data:
a catalogue record for this book is
available from the British Library

ISBN 978-1-4063-2422-8

www.walker.co.uk

This book is for Denise Johnstone-Burt,

who made me a real writer

Prologue

Nicolas de Mercadier

Fontevrault Abbey, Duchy of Anjou, 1152

I run for the tower, tearing through a tangle of lavender bushes. I need cover. I need to hide. Dried blood and tears dry on my face, on my neck, bitter salt on my lips. It hurts to move. My right-hand eye is swollen shut and my back is on fire. I'm gasping for breath, sweat pouring down my face as I look up. There's a window. It's cut deep into the tower wall high above me, the ledge in shadow. If only I could reach it I could hide up there, blending into that small patch of darkness.

I scramble up the mimosa tree, shaking loose great clouds of yellow blossom like flakes of sunlight; I climb the wall like a frantic spider, digging my fingers and my bare toes into whatever cracks in the stone face of the tower that I can find; higher, higher.

Don't look down.

I haul myself onto the window ledge; I can't breathe. I'm spent. *Oh, God, what if Anjou finds me?* I glance down into the chamber below, chest heaving. It's empty except for one long table set out down the middle, a bench on either side. The table is already laid with silver vessels and jugs, but there are no servants. The far wall is hung with tapestries. It's a long way down to the floor. I can't get down that way without breaking my neck.

And the nail-studded wooden door swings open.

It'll just be servants. Won't it?

It's not; it's Anjou himself, heir to the throne of England and my devil of a stepfather, still red and sweaty with the effort of blacking my eye and scourging the skin from my back – filthy, disgusting, sweating pig. My mother's at his side, her arm resting in the crook of his elbow. A surge of hatred boils through me when I see his face, him touching her. *Oh, God in heaven, don't look up.* Mama does: her eyes flicker towards the window ledge I'm sitting on, then away. She's seen me but this time she's chosen to preserve what's left of my hide. *Traitor.*

Still standing, Mama and Anjou wait in silence as a number of men step quietly into the room. The most corpse-like of them all is clad in the red habit of a cardinal. There is an abundance of golden chains, glossy bear hides, costly purple robes and ermine trimming – and yet not a single lackey. There's only one reason men cut of this cloth are prepared to pour their own wine and that's subterfuge.

Well done, Nicolas. You're hiding in a secret meeting crammed full of what looks very like the most rich and powerful collection of criminals in Christendom.

Anjou will definitely kill me now. It began when I looked at him the wrong way as I served my mother at fast-break, blew up like fire in the wind when my apology was "insolent", and now with a bloodied back and a fat black

8

eye I have stumbled on his treachery. If I'm caught, he'll kill me this day – if I don't crack open my head like a hen's egg falling from this windowsill before he gets the chance.

"How long must we wait?" The cardinal speaks in Latin, his voice thin and tired. He sounds a little afraid, and sweat trickles down between my shoulder blades. "Have you summoned us here as some kind of game, my lord Anjou, or do we really expect the guests you promised us?"

"Believe me, I'm serious." Anjou sounds as if he is on the edge of losing his temper – again. Mama is sitting very still and straight – this is no intimate gathering of friends.

And before anyone else can speak the air is full of white feathers, twisting and tumbling as if a goose-down bolster has burst open. The sweat chills on my back. Feathers: everywhere. All I can hear is the thin-voiced cardinal muttering a string of prayers and blood pounding in my ears. *Feathers.* They fly up past my face, whirling and soft, tickling my bare feet – so thick do they fall I can't see below me at all. What witchcraft is this? At last, the white cloud sinks to the floor, and now I see that this *is* no witchcraft. It's the Hidden, and I've never seen one of the Hidden in the flesh before. I've only ever heard the stories, the songs, and the breath freezes in my chest at the wonder of it.

There are four of them, tall and cloaked and more beautiful than any mortal, two girls and two boys, one much younger with wild red hair – a child, a Hidden child? I was always told the Hidden hatched full-grown from seething hot spawn spewed from the mouth of Hell. But here is a child who looks no older than me: thirteen. The other taller boy is wrapped in a cloak of swan's feathers that tangle in his black curls and pool around his feet. One of the girls is red-headed like the child, and the other's hair is silver-white like a pewter jug – I can't help noticing their hair, great swathes of it, shining and wild, not mortal, seeming to move and shimmer as if it is alive. Not one of the Hidden looks any more than three or four years older than I am – seventeen, maybe, but they could be much older than that. I drank these stories with my wet-nurse's milk: the Hidden don't age. They don't die unless you strike them with iron – they're cursed never to enter the kingdom of heaven. And they're *here*.

"What do you want, mortals of Fontevrault?" He of the feathered cloak speaks directly to Anjou, but his eyes are lingering on Mama, and a faint smile crosses his lips. I can't take my eyes away from them. There's something so familiar about the way they hold themselves: I've seen that strange, cat-like poise before—

Anjou doesn't reply, and I swallow the urge to laugh. He's scared of them. *Coward*.

"We want to strike a covenant with you." Mama stands, placing both hands palm-down on the table before her, and one of her rings glints in a shaft of light shining in through the window behind me. "Would any here dispute that our kind consorting with yours has its dangers?" Her voice is dry and calm, as if she is discussing the storage of winter linen.

The three full-grown Hidden share a swift glance but it's the cloaked one who speaks again, the swan-feathered boy, smiling as if these gathered noblemen and princes are nothing but foolish children. "Our longing for mortal

10

children, you mean?" he asks, very gently. "Or *your* longing for a drop of our immortal blood in your clans to make sure your rule is never shaken?" He sounds amused, as if on the verge of laughter.

"Both." Mama's voice rings out, and I know that tone. I wouldn't argue. I half want to laugh because this chamber is full of men – rulers – and they are all too afraid to speak to the Hidden. Even Anjou. The task is left to my mother.

The dark-haired Hidden boy shrugs, and the white feathers billow around his shoulders. "Very well, my lady. If we cannot live together, we shall live apart. If you do not come near us, the Hidden will grant you the same favour."

Just at that moment, the red-headed boy looks up. Right at me. For a thousand years, our eyes lock together, and I know that he's been where I am now – just a boy in boiling water up to his neck. He understands: if he's really the Devil's spawn then I am too, for we're the same. The Hidden boy looks away, back down at his white hands clasped together on the table, and my mouth is drier than the time Anjou stuffed it full of sand because I swore at him.

"Agreed," Mama says, her voice hard. "We will expunge the Hidden from all that is written: it shall be as if you were nothing but a tale to frighten children. My lords?"

But before they have a chance to speak, the white-haired girl smiles, and as one, every man in the room turns to look at her, as if somebody has just lit an oil lamp in a dark room.

"Are you quite sure," she says softly, "that there is not something you haven't told us, mortals? A detail you may have neglected to mention?"

And as I watch, Mama freezes, holding her hands utterly still and flat down on the table as if she is fighting the urge to hurl the nearest wine vessel at the girl and smash her beautiful face.

"Rose?" The boy in the feathered cloak throws his white-haired companion a glance I can't read the meaning of, and just as he does she makes a great show of looking up, right at the window where I am curled up into a ball, frozen with terror, on a narrow stone window ledge. The red-headed boy and girl glance at each other – she reaches out and places one hand over his, as if in protection. An older sister, perhaps?

All I can hear is the drumming of my heart.

One by one, the noblemen and the cardinal all follow the white-haired girl's gaze, some turning in their places on the bench to fix their eyes on me. Mama remains seated. She doesn't move. She doesn't even flinch. My legs burn with cramp, but I daren't move. If I fall from this ledge, I'll die – a bloody mess on the flagstones far below.

And then, last of all, Anjou turns. He stands, leaning back against the table, squinting against the sunlight streaming in through the window behind me, and I see new heights of rage in his eyes as some kind of understanding dawns. The chamber is silent. No one knows what to say. They all just watch me, and I'm sure that time has frozen and I will be trapped in this moment for ever, and softly – so softly – I swing one leg over the window ledge, ready to climb down the wall and run for my life.

And my stepfather says, "*Nicolas.*" The hatred in his voice hangs in the air like the stench of something rotting.

I'm not staying to finish this conversation.

And I slip. I can't hold on. Frantic, I scrabble for a grip on the windowsill but the stone is like oiled silk beneath my sweating hands and I really, *really* can't hold on—

I fall, I fall, and the ground rushes up to meet me so fast, and I crash through the mimosa tree, the lavender bushes, and the tearing agony of it becomes everything, and all is black.

PART ONE
A GIRL LOST IN TIME

1

Connie

"So are you coming tomorrow night, Amy? You could bring Mika in the pram." I knew it was a stupid thing to say the second I opened my mouth. Even wrapped in the enormous patchwork blanket I'd spent three months knitting, Mika was still smaller than the Creed family's ancient and bad-tempered calico cat. There was no way Amy was going to bring her newborn to a party in the woods.

"Not this time, Connie." Amy grinned at me, adjusting the blanket around Mika's tiny body – she never seemed to mind my ignorance, even though I was three and a half years younger. She was in this total haze. Whacked out on baby hormones. "Mum used to take me and Blue everywhere when we were babies, though," she went on. "We had these special earphones for festivals and we slept in a wheelbarrow. She says there's no reason why my life has to grind to a halt just because of Mika." For a second Amy looked worried. "She's already on at me about when I'm going to start my course again. I just don't know how I'm going to fit everything in." Amy paused. She always knew just what I was thinking. "You look really tired, Con. Are you not

17

sleeping? It's that time of year again, isn't it?"

I shrugged. For me, early-summer would never be about a new season, a fresh beginning. When the nights grew longer, I always thought of Lissy, and how she wasn't there. But what could I say?

Amy reached out and took hold of my hand, twisting her fingers around mine. "I never really knew your sister. You must miss her so much. I mean, Blue's a total pain, but if he wasn't there it'd just be so weird and wrong. And your brother hardly ever comes home."

I was glad she hadn't said Lissy's name. Even now, six years later, I still couldn't bear the sound of her name.

I had to look away for a second or else I was going to cry. "Look, you should come on Friday!" I sounded too bright, too fake. "We can get Mika some teeny ear defenders. Your mum's right. Mika's gorgeous and amazing, but he's no excuse to sit around at home for the rest of your life."

Amy just raised both eyebrows at me, accepting without argument the fact that I didn't want to talk about my dead sister any more than she wanted to think about resuming normal life. "Don't you know the ancient legends, Connie Harker?" She spoke in an exaggerated stage whisper. "You must never, ever take a newborn baby within a mile of Hopesay Reach."

I rolled my eyes again. "Ri–ight. Or the fairies will come and take him away. I've heard all the stories, Ames. And anyway, Blue told me that Nye was going to set up his sound system over in the woods so we don't get the Hopesay zombies calling the police – you won't have to bring Mika anywhere near the House of Horrors."

Amy grinned. "I'm not worried about the scary fairies, Con, you know that. I love the Reach, and they're only stories. I'm just tired, that's all. You and Blue will have an amazing time."

I glanced out of the window. It was getting dark. Right on cue Amy's younger brother stuck his head around the door, white-blond hair flopping into his eyes as usual, the sleeves of his favourite faded old lumberjack shirt rolled up to the elbows. There were some things I could only talk about with Amy but at school me and Blue were always together, just like we'd been since I first came to live at Hopesay Edge. It had been such a dark, confusing time. All those weeks I'd spent in hospital, so weak, knowing that when I finally got out, Lissy just wasn't going to be there.

"Con, Mum's heading into town. Do you want a lift? She doesn't want you walking home in the dark." Blue rolled his eyes at the over-protectiveness, but despite his piss-taking I knew Mrs Creed was deadly serious. It really was getting dark, shadows lengthening down the lawn, and she never liked letting me walk home alone, superstitious just like everyone else in Hopesay Edge. Blue stepped in, bringing with him the faint, warm scent of the spices his mum had been making him grind in the kitchen – cumin seeds and turmeric.

He shut the door behind him. "So when are they going? Your mum and Nick? They're definitely going, right?"

His excitement was infectious and I couldn't help grinning back. "Yes, Blue – my great-aunt's still dead and they're off in the morning. Which means that tomorrow night we're still having the most legendary party of all time."

Amy frowned. "They're away for nearly a week, aren't they? Are you going to be all right hanging around in the Reach by yourself, Con? Why don't you come and stay here?"

I half wanted to laugh, because the solution Mum and Nick had come up with to that little problem was all so unbelievably awful: *Joe, Joe, Joe.* "Don't worry, I've got a babysitter. My stepbrother's coming in the morning. I'll be fine without a lift, but tell your mum thanks anyway." Joe. *Oh, God.* I got up, slipping on a battered red sweatshirt that had once belonged to my brother – Rafe wasn't likely to demand it back. He hadn't been home in five years. I guess if I were teaching hot gap-year students how to dive in India, Hopesay Edge wouldn't be much of a draw to me, either. I blew kisses at Amy and Mika, then turned to Blue. "I'll see you in the morning, loser." I punched him in the ribs just hard enough and left by the back door before Mrs Creed got serious. The last thing I wanted was a ride home with Amy and Blue's mum firing questions at me the whole time about what I was going to do with myself while Mum and Nick were away.

Running down the long strip of garden, I left the black-and-white timbered cottage behind – lit-up windows warm and yellow against the gathering darkness – and I actually sprinted past the neat rows of tiny early-summer onions and carrots in case Mrs Creed decided it was too dark after all and called me back.

I climbed the stile at the end of the Creeds' garden and hopped down into long wet grass. This was the oldest part of the churchyard and all the graves here were pretty ancient, the stone dotted with pale green circles of lichen, names all worn away, with no one to remember them. It was so quiet. Lissy wasn't buried in Hopesay Edge. Mum, Dad and Rafe had scattered her ashes off the headland near Granny's house by the sea. Aged nine, I'd refused to go – that was back when I still didn't believe that Lissy was really dead. Before I'd accepted the truth: she was never coming back. She was just gone.

I ran through the churchyard, feathery fronds of grass sticking to my bare legs, unable to believe that it was really happening and Mum and Nick were actually leaving me with Joe. I mean, so at least this meant he'd never told them what I'd done at Christmas, but I really had no idea how I was going to face him again without actually dying of shame.

I had to stop running and just stand there among the gravestones and horse-chestnut trees, forcing myself to relive the night I'd sneaked out of the holiday cottage: anything to escape Mum and Nick's awful Christmas Eve drinks party, all those leering drunken middle-aged people breathing salmon-breath into my face. And then Joe following me down to the waterfront, jaunty coloured Christmas lights hanging between the street lights and even twinkling on the boats bobbing up and down in the harbour. I used to get so excited about going to the cottage every Christmas. Not any more.

Joe had sat down on the wall beside me. *You're pissed, aren't you? Bloody hell, Connie, you're only thirteen.*

Fourteen. I'm fourteen. I'd stared out at the black, glittering sea beyond the harbour wall, trying to ignore the way those bobbing fairy lights made me feel sick. *Don't tell me you never got drunk when you were my age.*

Yeah, but I used to do stuff like this with my mates. Drinking on your own isn't a good sign, Con. In fact, it's a really, really bad sign.

I'd turned to stare at him, at the chocolatey brown hair falling over his face, those high cheekbones. *If you weren't so gorgeous, I'd be angry with you, you know? Stop interfering, all right?*

Joe had shot me an incredulous look. *Shut up, Connie. You don't know what you're saying. Look, come on back to the cottage and we'll get you some water. If you're quick we can get back before anyone knows you've gone.*

Don't be stupid, Joe. I could stay out all night and they still wouldn't notice. Mum wouldn't, anyway. And I hadn't been able to stop myself. Hadn't really wanted to stop myself, to tell the truth. I just watched my hand reaching out as if it belonged to someone else and I could do nothing to prevent it landing on Joe's knee. The rough, warm feel of his jeans, the fabric of my skirt glittering silver and red under the street lights. It was me. I really was touching him.

You're just so lovely, Joe.

He'd jerked away like I'd slapped him, his face stiff with horror. *What are you doing, Connie? I'm six years older than you.*

You're the only one who gives a shit about me, you know. The only one.

Joe slid sideways along the wall, putting as much distance between us as he could, pity written all over his face. *Listen,*

Con. One day you're going to make a lucky bloke really happy, but you're fourteen and I'm your stepbrother, OK? This is wrong. Really, really wrong. Come on, let's get you back to the house.

His pity was the worst thing, and I think that's what made me angry enough to say it: *Don't give me that stepbrother bullshit. I'm fourteen and I'm not Lissy. That's the most important thing, isn't it? You were her stepbrother, too. **I'm not Lissy.** She's dead, Joe. Get over it.*

He'd walked away then, without another word, and I'd stayed out all night, and no one came to find me, because no one else gave enough of a crap, and I'd pushed Joe just about as far as it was possible to push him.

I sat down among the gravestones, covering my face with my hands as if I could somehow shove away the memory. I'd made a move on Joe – on my own stepbrother – and now I had to live with him for an entire week. Knowing that he had to be dreading it as much as I was really didn't help. I couldn't help shivering, suddenly unable to shake the feeling that someone was actually watching me, a witness to my melodramatic collapse.

You really just can't stop embarrassing yourself, can you, Connie Harker? It'll be a dog walker, I told myself sternly. *A dog walker who now probably thinks I'm crazy. Loads of people go this way.* There was a public footpath running across the southernmost corner of the orchard at home and now that Uncle Miles was gone people had started using it again, climbing over the stile in the churchyard right into the grounds of the Reach.

But that didn't explain why the temperature had dropped five degrees, cold air biting through my thin sweatshirt. The skin on the back of my neck tingled like the time Blue quietly pushed a handful of sheep's wool he'd untangled from a barbed-wire fence down the back of my T-shirt and I'd nearly wet myself shrieking. *Run!* I screamed at myself. I couldn't move. My legs just wouldn't obey my brain and I couldn't get up. *Pull yourself together, Connie.* Swallowing my fear, I forced myself back up onto my feet and stood still among the tumbled and silent rows of headstones, goosebumps rising on my legs.

There it was again, that prickling, uneasy sensation of being *watched*. Bright pain spasmed behind my eyes, and I rubbed my temples. Another headache, just like I always got when I woke up after the Dream. I didn't want to think about the Dream now. Not here. Wind shifted the branches of the huge, spreading old horse-chestnut trees, releasing the heady scent of their blossom.

"Hello?" I shouted. "Is anyone there? Come on. Stop messing with me." I did my best to sound tough and unafraid, but my heartbeat wouldn't stop accelerating, and despite that chill in the air a cool trickle of sweat slid down my back.

No reply. All I could hear was birdsong and the rustle of wind in the trees shaking loose pale slivers of horse-chestnut blossom that drifted around me like snow, catching in my hair.

"Don't be an idiot," I said, aloud. "There's no one here but you. You're not getting enough sleep, that's all. Imagining stuff."

I ran, heart pounding in my chest, cutting through the churchyard until I pushed my way through the gap in the

24

hedge that led to the safety of our orchard – *home* – a glorious tangle of crabbed and twisted apple trees. The chickens had all been put away, which was usually my job, but it was still light – just – so Mum couldn't hold *that* against me, at least.

Winding my way through the apple trees, I stepped out onto the lawn, breathing in the gorgeous warm green scent of cut grass and the rich muddiness of the lake. The Reach sprawled beyond the carpet of lawn: a tumbling mass of warm stone, ancient timbers and a hundred mismatched windows. The sky was a swirling mass of fiery sunset, all reflected in the lake like it was the window to another world. I stood for a moment, my cold unease in the churchyard all forgotten, just drinking in the beauty of it all. It was funny to think how much I'd hated the Reach when we first came: it was here that Lissy had died. In time, though, I'd come to love every twisted chimney and every ancient door, which was proof, I suppose, of the Reach's power – a sure sign that I should have been more cautious.

2
Joe

Garsdale, North Yorkshire

It was pissing it down on Mab's Top just like bloody always – thick grey cloud right down to the ring of standing stones, hanging wet cloud so low I could hardly see the grass. It was June and just before nightfall, the sun too weak to break open the mist. It was murder, this weather, and if I'd known it'd tip down like this I'd have come with a Maglite. I had to kick around in the grass for the sheep-trough till I heard the clang of galvanized metal against the toe of my boot before I could tip in the sack of feed. I knew I should be getting back to the house with that god-awful drive ahead of me in the morning, but I couldn't help walking up the hill.

The stones reared up out of the mist, silent and creepy, covered in scabby moss: huge great things, just waiting there on the fellside. Grandad always called them the Dancers. When I reached out to touch the nearest one, it was warm against my fingertips, like it'd soaked up the sun all day. Except that there'd been no sun, not for weeks. Another wet summer, like the one Lissy left behind six years ago. I spread my fingers out till my palm rested against the rain-wet stone. Warm, like they were alive.

I always felt nearer to Lissy up by the Dancers. I shut my eyes and saw her face, that red hair. *She's trapped and I let Rafe and Adam do it. We let the Swan King take her down into the Halls of the Hidden. Jesus Christ, Lissy. I'm sorry. We should have found another way, but he'd got us backed into such a bloody corner, hadn't he? He demanded Lissy's freedom in exchange for Connie's life.*

What else could we have done? I'd paid for that choice every second of my life since the morning Lissy stepped into the lake at Hopesay Reach and walked out of the world and into the Halls of the Hidden. I failed every exam I ever took after that day, like my brain was just scrambled. Addled. Every time I closed my eyes I saw her face, and no matter how much I drank or whatever else I could get my hands on she was always, always there. The second I closed my eyes. Out of reach, trapped. It was my fault. I should have stopped them: I should have done something.

Get out of here, Joe, I told myself, furious. *Walk down to the quad. Get back down to the house. Wherever Lissy is, whatever she's doing, she's probably forgotten you even exist. It's a joke. Your life's a bloody joke.*

For six years I'd managed to keep away from the Reach, out of temptation's way. When Dad asked me to babysit Connie for a week, what was I meant to say? *Sorry, I can't – I'm too scared that she's going to jump me.* They'd not told her about Lissy, either, afraid that knowing might put her in the way of the Fontevrault. But all lies are like ticking bombs waiting to go off, whatever the reason behind them. It's a right shame the Fontevrault had to look so bloody normal, because everywhere I went, I could never be sure they weren't there. Watching me to make sure I stayed well away from the Gateway, from the Hidden. *Following*. It's not paranoia when they really are out to get you.

What a crap-heap of a mess. Slipping on the wet grass and hemmed with fog, I cursed all the way back down the hillside, desperate to get off the fell as fast as I could. The Reach was calling me already. Lissy was calling me. She must've known I'd always come, no matter what.

3

Lissy

Halls of the Hidden

I sense the sudden rush of air half a second too late. The dart whistles past my ear, burying itself deep into my forearm. Bright pain explodes and blood wells up around the protruding silver shaft, warm against my skin. Sucking in a breath of air, I screw a lid down on my fury and yank the dart from my flesh, squeezing my eyes shut against bright hot pain. I whirl around to face another dart hurtling towards me but this time I'm quick enough to duck faster than any ordinary human can even think, and the dart clatters to the ground, a shard of silver at my feet.

The White Hall is empty, save me. A vast, glittering chamber gouged out of solid quartz. There is no one here. Nobody to throw the darts.

No one I can see, anyway. He is here, though. I know he is. Heart pounding, I wait.

"Too slow, Lissy." Impossibly, the Swan King is in the White Hall even though I can't see him. My father. Impossibly, he is also now behind me.

I whirl around again, and now I'm face to face with him – he's taller than I am, dark, silvery eyes watching me, the white feathers of his cloak brushing his cheek, so pale against the black hair spilling around his shoulders. Quick as a snake, he reaches out and takes hold of my wrist, pulling me closer. I gasp at the chill of his touch and we both look down at the blood, so bright against my skin. The wound is already healing, broken flesh knitting itself back together, my skin smooth once more, stained with a faint silvery scar and dark blood which is neither truly human nor truly Hidden. Not that this stops it hurting. I heal, but that does not lessen the sting.

He gives me a faint, incredulous smile. "I caught you. Why did you let me?"

I grant him no reply; I fling the dart straight at his face instead. Smiling again, he holds up one hand and it simply drops clean out of the air and clatters, harmless, on the cold white rock at our feet. He reaches out to me and I flinch in anticipation of the blow, but instead my father only touches my face with gentle delicacy, as if brushing his fingers against the cheek of a newborn child.

"You're a fool," he whispers. "When it comes to the last battle, win the fight, Lissy. If my hand fails and the Fontevrault catch you, you'll know imprisonment worse even than this. You'll never receive the gift of death. If you would have mastery over yourself, use it as you ought to. Try again, Lissy."

I feel the chill of hard metal against my neck. My eyes shift to the left, and he's holding the bronze knife from the scabbard at his waist right against my bare skin – he can move so very, very fast. With every last shred of willpower, I glance up at the dizzying white reaches of the cavern far above us;

I focus my mind, forcing myself to forget the possibility of being held prisoner by the Fontevrault if I ever free myself from here, the threat of escaping one form of imprisonment only to find myself trapped again.

Fly.

An electric tingling spreads across my skin as I take on my hawk-form – and I am no longer standing, no longer even touching the ground at all but beating my hawk-wings, soaring hard away till at last I'm looking down on the Swan King, a black-haired figure far below, his cloak of white feathers trailing on the ground at his feet, face upturned as he watches my flight. He holds out one arm – the command for me to come – and for just a few seconds I allow myself the dangerous liberty of disobeying him, circling and soaring around the cavern under the illusion of freedom.

I'm no fool. I descend at my father's unspoken command, landing on his outstretched wrist, my hawk-talons scoring lines of silvery-blue Hidden blood against his pale skin that fade to nothing in the time it takes for me to shape-change again and step to the ground, a girl once more.

He smiles again. "Better. I have lost count of the times I've wished that flight was not only the royal gift of the Hidden, that all our tribe could fly free from mortal danger. Lissy, if the Fontevrault ever catch you, you'll be their prisoner till the world crumbles into dust and you are the only one left alive. If the mortal race find out what you are, Lissy, that you are even possible, they will drain every drop of your Hidden blood for a taste of immortality. The Fontevrault will use you as a breeding machine, as an experiment. So don't fail me again, daughter. I have lost so many already. All those I loved so very much. Don't be amongst them."

Fury flashes through me. "You're no one to talk about using girls. What about Tippy?" Grief punches through me as I recall the day I first found her, just a little mortal girl-child kept prisoner by the Hidden, running around the endless tunnels in the ragged old nightie she'd been wearing when Rose stole her three hundred years before, how pathetically *grateful* Tippy had been as I brushed the tangles from her hair, neglected for so long. She'd given up her life to grant me the chance of freedom. All for nothing. I can't drain the anger from my voice, even though I know speaking to my father in such a way is unwise to say the least: "Tippy was desperate. Desperate to see her family again. You kept her for three centuries hoping eventually that she'd grow up and you'd be able to use her like some kind of breeding cow." I don't dare mention Iris and the other victims of my father's desire for revenge on the mortals. "You didn't *lose* Larkspur, either – you exiled him. It was your choice."

He's been watching me with an infuriating amused smile, but the second Larkspur's name tumbles from my lips all control leaves him, replaced with sudden naked fury. He reaches out to strike me and I duck; he grabs my wrist, his touch spreading a deep cold that freezes me where I stand. We remain face to face. My heart throbs, pounding and pounding; I look up at him, expecting to be hurled halfway across the White Hall. He's done it before. He could break every bone in my body without lifting a finger, without so much as touching me. He does not. We stare at each other, the world continuing to move around us as all the while we are still. I've never once seen the Swan King shed a tear, but the dark emptiness in his eyes is worse. God knows, I swear I can almost feel his despair – so deep and relentless, such endless longing. First he lost Larkspur's mother, and then finally Larkspur himself. Now I see the truth: it's almost too much for the Swan King to bear.

"Don't make me hurt you. I don't want to." He drops my wrist, eyes locked on mine. "Don't speak of Larkspur again, Lissy. Please."

Don't make me hurt you? As if it's my fault.

"It doesn't have to be like this." I'm breathless and terrified, but the words spill out before I can stop them. Nothing can bring back Larkspur's mother, but is there not still hope for my brother? "Larkspur would come if you called him. He'd be here before dawn. He'd go down on his knees for you. All you have to do is ask."

The Swan King smiles, bittersweet. "But you, my half-breed daughter, are the only one with the power to let him in. And yet you refuse to open the Gateway. Time and time again you have refused."

"Then don't release the plague. Promise you won't."

He laughs, gently releasing my wrist. "How could you trust me, Lissy? How could you be sure I wouldn't do it? You made one bargain with me, daughter, and that should have taught you never to attempt another."

I shrug, choosing my words with utmost care. "It's true you've outmanoeuvred me before. But what if you proved I could trust you?"

He smiles again. I've amused him once more – his entertaining little toy. "And how, my own darling, my Hidden Princess, how would I earn your trust?"

"My blood," I reply, before I have the sense to shut up. "You took it. You used it to make the plague. Destroy the silver vial – destroy the plague – and I'll open the Gateway. It's all you have to do. I'll release you and Larkspur will come. You know he will."

We're standing so close I can see the steady rise and fall of his chest as he breathes, the white feathers of his cloak shivering and shifting with each soft movement. When he speaks, his voice is so sweet that I want to cry. "But who would stop me cutting your throat, darling one, the moment you opened the Gateway? Even if I destroyed the vial before your eyes, Lissy, your blood is not so very difficult to come by."

"Why don't you just let it all go?" I say, quietly, not even caring what he does to me now. How long must we go on like this, deadlocked? "Why make the mortals suffer so much for a crime not one of them committed? Even the Fontevrault who killed Larkspur's mother have been dead for centuries. The plague won't punish them, only the innocent."

"I betrayed her once," he says, never taking his eyes from mine. "I should have been at her side; I should have saved her life. What can I do but honour her memory, Lissy?"

"You don't need to honour her memory with blood," I whisper. We're standing so close I feel the sweet warmth of his breath on my face. "Honour it with love."

And for just the briefest moment, the hardness in his eyes

softens, and I see my father as I've never seen him before – a wild and beautiful creature, full of compassion, and a tiny flame of hope stirs inside me. Have I found my way out of this prison, at last? But my father says nothing; he just turns and walks away, the cloak of white feathers trailing along the ground behind him, silent as a fall of snow.

He leaves with no promises, and I'm afraid. One day, sooner or later, the Swan King will find a way to end his imprisonment in the White Hall of the Hidden, whether that's by forcing me to open the Gateway, or some other more complicated trick, less easy to combat. And when that day comes, he will spread a plague from one end of the earth to the other that will destroy every last man, woman and child – unless I can find a way of stopping him.

4

Larkspur

Sahara Desert, Morocco

Stars prickle the desert night. It's getting cold even though the heat was searing just a few hours ago, and I wrap the cloak closer about my shoulders. In my mind I'm centuries away from this sea of sand, this quiet darkness, back to the morning I stood with my father at the foot of a tower with the sun hammering against my head, looking down at a boy lying face-down in the dust. The back of his white chemise was thick with dried blood – I remember wondering at the thick dark richness of his blood.

"So cruel, Larkspur," my father said to me. "The mortals beat their young; they break their skin." And he crouched down at the boy's side, the white feathers of his cloak puddling in the dirt. "Get up," he said in our own Hidden tongue, a language no ordinary mortal could possibly understand. The second test – Nicolas had already survived a fall that would have killed a mortal. "Get up now, Nicolas de Mercadier."

The boy turned his head to the side and his eyes snapped open. More dark blood leaked from his ear, a glossy trickle across dusty earth and grit. *Nicolas.*

"Am I in Hell?" He thought he was dead, yet there was

no trace of fear on his face, and I remember wondering if his life was so miserable he would really rather be dead. With a small moan like a hound with a thorn in its pad, he turned to lie on his side, still looking up at us. His gaze travelled from my father to me and back again, still without a trace of fear.

"I said, get up." My father reached out with one hand and hauled Nicolas to his feet; his bloodied face screwed itself into knots of agony, but my father paid no attention to that.

"Who are you?" Nicolas coughed, spitting blood into the dust at his feet. Despite the fearless look in his eyes, he was trembling all over now; he kept clenching his hands into fists but every time his fingers unfurled they were still shaking.

My father smiled. "Listen to me, Nicolas. Anjou married your mother knowing she had a bastard child hidden at Fontevrault Abbey, but had he known what manner of bastard you are, all the gold in Christendom would not have been enough to tempt him. Thanks to my sister Rose and her loose tongue, Anjou now knows exactly what you are — what your mother has smuggled into his family."

"What do you mean, what I am?"

I remember being so astonished at his audacity, interrupting the Swan King. But Nicolas seemed more interested in staring down in disbelief at his bloodied clothes than being afraid of anything, as if amazed that his legs were still holding him upright. He was a headstrong fool then, and so he is now.

My father only smiled again. "We have so little time. There is a tale for the telling, Nicolas, but not now. If you want to save your mother's life, then come with us, and run."

He took no more convincing. My father took one of his arms, and I the other, and we ran as far from the traitorous mortals of Fontevrault as we could, deep into the forest.

A memory bursts across my mind, sharp and bright, the smell of leaf mould, streams of sunlight lancing down between the trees, spring-water rushing over moss-covered rocks. *Come, Larkspur*, my mother had said and we both held out our cupped hands, gathering water so cold that I gasped, carrying it to the place where Nicolas sat hunched at the foot of a larch tree, the blood-stained chemise in a filthy heap at his feet. My father and Rose stood watching him to be sure this new prize would not run, and we tipped water down his back till it ran in rivulets between his shoulder blades, coursing over the ridges of broken, bleeding skin, and Nicolas never once made a sound.

Crouching at his side with tears in her eyes, my mother looked up at my father. *My own love, get the child water for his face.*

In all the world, she was the only one whose word he ever obeyed. My father went to the stream himself, and crouching before Nicolas so that the white feathers of his cloak grew tangled in larch needles, he poured the water into Nicolas's outstretched hands. Nicolas glanced up at him, his dark mortal eyes fierce and wild as a cat's, and he splashed his face till the water flew out in drops that caught the last of the sunlight like old pearls. Because of that, we did not see him weep. Because of that, Nicolas became my father's most devoted slave, and I his brother, even though we were bound only by the blood I helped him wash away, not by the blood in our veins. It may have been more than eight hundred years ago, that morning, yet I can still smell sun-warmed lavender mixed with the heat of Nicolas's half-mortal blood: the son of a long-dead medieval queen and a Hidden lord killed with an iron blade before his miraculous child even drew breath. More mortal treachery.

And silent, I walk across the desert sand, leaving no trace behind, unlike the mortal nomads and their livestock who have left a churn of prints that will be all blown to nothing by the wind once they have packed up their camp and moved on.

The cluster of tents is quiet and dark, all campfires extinguished save one. His. I hear the soft breathing of animals, of people. A child lets out a swift cry, quickly stilled. I stand, waiting. I can't be seen. Not with Nicolas. It's too dangerous. Alone, he can just about move amongst ordinary mortals undetected. Not with me.

He is awake; I know he is. I sense that he is nearby. I follow the faint glow of the banked-down flames.

I find Nicolas sitting outside a tent furthest from the others, just watching the stars. They've never changed, not in all the long years he's walked this earth alone. He looks away from the fire's glow to see me coming, and my heart lifts to see that swift, rare smile.

"Larkspur." He embraces me, but pulls away with a frown. "What in Hell's name are you doing here? It's too dangerous."

I sit down beside him on the pile of rugs, glancing back at the tent. "Have you a woman inside?"

"Shut up." Nicolas passes me a glass of steaming tea

that scalds my fingertips. It tastes of sunlight: mint and hot sweetness. "I'm serious. You know the risks. Why have you come?"

I turn a little, just so I can watch his eyes, the dark hair falling around his face. "You know why I'm here, Nico. I've seen her in the water, too."

Nicolas looks away, back up at the stars. "Who is she? I see her all the time. *All the time.*"

I know he's afraid, and in all the long years I've known him, he's only ever been afraid of losing me. Or my father. I sling one arm around his shoulder. The fire's still smouldering but it's not throwing out enough heat. "Show me what you see, Nico. Who do you see?"

"Watch out – iron." As if he needs to warn me. The faint stink of it on the air is enough to curdle my belly. Nicolas leans forwards and plucks the iron pot out of the fire with his bare fingers. He's withstood enough pain over the last nine hundred years that a little of it doesn't matter to him any more. Just because he can't die, it doesn't mean that several different mortals haven't gone their length to kill him, kings and princes all – including his own stepfather.

Nicolas blows on his fingers with a whispered curse and sets the pot down on the ground at our feet. Water sloshes over the pot's rim, staining the sand. He glances at me. "*Look.*"

I obey, fixing my eyes on the water – it's slightly oily, as if he's cooked meat in here: for all his long life, Nicolas still has some odd mortal traits. I wait, listening to his heartbeat quicken as the water's skin darkens and takes on a strange glassy sheen, as if the grease thickens before our eyes. And now I see her, too: a girl lying asleep, golden hair spread all over her white pillow, her lips slightly parted.

It's what I feared the most.

Nicolas has seen Connie, Lissy's sister. She's Tainted and it's my fault. My father has been planning his revenge on the mortals for so long and now, thanks to me, Connie is just what he needs to escape the Halls.

I push away the memory of mortal figures rushing at my mother and me in the woods beyond Fontevrault Abbey, a mortal man snatching my mother, holding her close to his body. The thick cross-hatch of coarse dark hairs on his forearm. Her eyes spilling tears as she looked at me one last time, the endless silence as she crumpled to the ground into the leaves, blood spilling from her slit throat, her red hair fanning out around her as she lay on the ground like one of Tippy's broken dolls.

I remember Nicolas dropping to his knees at my father's feet, his chemise still stained with blood from the whip-cuts on his back, my father's cloak of white swan feathers still blackened with my mother's blood. There was blood everywhere, *everywhere*, and still I hear the wild desperation in Nicolas's voice: *It's my fault the mortals killed her. Anjou was so angry. I'll go, I'll go—* And my father just looked down at him and said, *You will not go. This was a mortal crime, and I will make them pay. They will all pay, Nicolas.*

And now I fear that after almost nine hundred years, my father might be on the edge of exacting that payment at long last, and I'm to blame. Lissy's got mortal blood – she could pass through the Gateway any time she chose and remove every single last iron cross at the Reach to allow my father and the rest of the Hidden out of the Halls, but she knows what the consequences would be. She's been strong-willed enough to refuse – so far. But Connie's just a mortal girl, and I'm willing to wager that she has no idea what she's dealing with – what my father's true nature is. If the Swan King has made contact with Connie, if he's persuaded her to open the Gateway and he escapes to release his plague, the fault will be all mine. I should have let Connie Harker die six years ago.

5

Connie

"Let me out. Oh, my darling, let me out…"

My Dream is always the same: surrounded by darkness with no end and no beginning, deep and endless. And then, of course, the Voice. Again.

"Let me out. Open it. Just for me. Come on—"

He sounds so pleading and desperate, but there's still something warm and irresistible in his voice and I'd do anything to see his face. I've got to save him; I've got to let him out of this dark prison, but I can never find him.

"Where are you?" I cry.

All I hear in reply is the faint sound of laughter.

But this time, there's something different, too – a silver light glowing in the distance. Hope. I run towards it as hard and as fast as I can, and the closer I get to the light the more the darkness begins to make sense. I glimpse details – the wet shine of a rock wall. Small stones crunching beneath my bare feet. A cave. I'm in some kind of underground cave— And he's close. So very, very close—

"Stop. Stop where you are."

And I look up to see Lissy blocking my path, looking down at me with an odd expression on her face – a weird mixture of fury and tenderness. When she speaks, though, she sounds exactly the same as ever: "Don't, Connie. Don't interfere. Please, it's so important. Stay away from here."

My sister. My dead sister.

And when Lissy reaches out to touch my face, her fingertip is so cold that I gasp. She's even taller than I remember, dressed in a ragged pearl-silver gown that clings to her white shoulders, her narrow lean body. All that beautiful red hair hangs down past her waist now, just as if she wasn't really dead and it's carried on growing.

"Let me go," I say, urgent. "You can't stop me. You have to help. He needs help. There's someone trapped down here, a boy. With you. Lissy, please—"

But all she says is, "You must not pass." Like some ancient queen from a story. And I can do nothing but reach out for her cold, cold hands.

"Come home," I beg. "Will you please just come home? I'm so lonely, Lissy. Mum hasn't been the same since you left – no one has."

She smiles, so wild and beautiful, my sister, and there are tears sliding down her white face. And all the same, she says no. She always, always says no—

6

Lissy

Halls of the Hidden

I can't breathe. *Thank God he is gone, thank God, thank God, thank God—*

I can only stare. I crouch on cold white stone, a hand's breadth from the still waters of the Gateway. Still breathless, I glance over my shoulder to make sure I'm alone. The walls of the White Hall glitter at me in silence, and there is no sign of the Swan King. He's gone – he's really gone—

This ought to be my reflection staring back at me from the water but instead of my own face, I see another: full eyebrows – straight and dramatic – a darker shade of gold than her hair, golden-brown skin and eyes like chips of green glass. She has changed, though. Grown. *Connie.* Five years older than when I last saw her, perhaps even six. She's about fourteen, then. The age I was when everything changed: that dangerous time. Seven and seven again, when the barrier between the mortal world and other places abrades: it's like an old sheet worn translucent in the middle when you hold it up to the light.

Tears dry on my cheeks and my skin feels tight as a drum, tingling. Relentless cold moves up through the ancient rock, chilling my bare feet.

It really is her. Connie. My little sister. How is she doing this – why am I able to see her? Connie stares at me, her green eyes unblinking, glistening with unshed tears. She was never one to cry easily. Her lips move, but I can't hear her voice. She's so lovely – I wonder if she's had a first boyfriend yet, and what her friends are like.

What is she trying to tell me?

"Connie! You must not pass," I whisper again, frantic with the fear that we might be discovered, that my father might suddenly step from the shadows – but the image of her face shivers, as if a breeze has ruffled the surface of the water, even though I know as well as anyone else that the air never moves in the Halls of the Hidden. The waters shiver and shift and Connie fades until she is nothing but a memory. *But she was here.* I saw her face. My little sister. I can't stop crying, tears just streaming down my face because the truth is I can never go home, no matter how much I want to.

And if *I've* seen my sister in the waters of the Gateway, peering into the White Hall like an uninvited guest pressing their nose against the window-pane at a party, then who else has Connie shown herself to? My father? Does the Swan King know that Connie has found a way of peering into the Halls of the Hidden, a mortal girl with the power to open the Gateway? My father spends more time alone in the White Hall than anyone. Who is to say that he has not seen Connie's reflection staring back at him instead of his own? She is mortal, immune to the iron magic that seals the Gateway, and unlike me, I would be willing to bet that Connie has no idea what will happen if she does open it.

What if he persuades her to try?

7

Connie

Hopesay Reach

I woke in a sweaty panic, sitting up in bed as I gathered the duvet around my bare shoulders. It was late – very late – and my head throbbed. Headaches like that only ever came after the Dream of the boy – only ever the Voice, so desperate and lonely. And now Lissy, too. I'd dreamed of her so many times since she died – flashbacks to all the thousands of memories we shared: reading together, running along a beach in Cornwall with her hair flying out like a bright flag against the blue sky – but this was different. She *looked* different. Taller, with all that hair. *And trapped in that dark, dark place…*

I hit the light switch, flooding my bedroom with comforting yellow light from the blue-and-white painted china lamp I'd had since I was five. *Jesus, Connie. Get a grip.* I reached for the packet of aspirin at my bedside and chewed up three of them, a bitter and chalky mess. It hurt to swallow. How many hours had it been since I'd left Mum and Nick to faff over their packing and come up to bed with a Marmite sandwich and Nick's cinnamon-spiked cocoa? The cup and plate had disappeared from my bedside table, so one of them must have looked in after I'd fallen asleep. They'd gone to bed now, though. The house was quiet. I was alone. There was no point in calling out. How would I even explain this to them, anyway? Where would I even begin? *I have dreams that feel so real. Too real.* I didn't want to go back to Deborah the Counsellor with her dyed purple hair and questionable standards of personal hygiene. I'd spent long enough with her after Lissy died.

My sister's not really dead. I know she's not.

What makes you think that, Connie? I could still see the carefully manufactured look of concern on Deborah's face.

I don't know. I just know, that's all.

No one had understood then. No one would understand now, and now it was even worse — Lissy was actually talking to me in my sleep, the tip of her finger so cold against my face. So real. Who could I talk to about this? Who could I tell? Nobody would believe me.

"Face it, Connie —" I switched off the lamp, whispering to the darkness — "you're in this alone." I don't even know how long I sat leaning against my pillows, watching the moonlight slant into my room through the diamond-leaded window, tipping a silver puddle onto the floorboards My eyes travelled to the iron cross nailed above the curtain rail. There was a crucifix above every window at Hopesay Reach, and one above every single door, black iron.

Why don't we just take them down? I'd said to Mum one day. *They give me the creeps.* And Mum told me that if we did, no one from the village would ever come here to do the cleaning for us, which was enough of a deterrent for me. I didn't care what rubbish the zombies in Hopesay Edge believed — if it

49

meant I didn't have to scour rusty old bathtubs and brush cobwebs from every corner of a house big enough to get lost in, the freaky iron crosses could stay. There was something strangely reassuring about them, anyway, solid and ageless in the cold moonlight. With the headache still pulsing behind my eyes, I kept my eyes on the crucifix till at last I knew I was falling asleep again, as if in some stupid way an old iron cross might offer protection.

It's just a dream, Connie, I told myself, fierce with anger at how much it had frightened me, like a little child scared of a nightmare. But no matter how much I tried to convince myself, I knew the Voice was more than just a dream.

In my heart, I knew the Voice was real, that someone was desperately trying to get me to listen. And that was why it scared me so much.

8

Lissy

Halls of the Hidden

Connie. I stare at the black water, but she has gone, as if she were never there, as if I imagined the whole thing, and perhaps I did. Perhaps I have been a prisoner so long that my mind is starting to crack right open. Six years would be long enough, would it not, with the threat of my father's revenge hanging over me the whole time? An unravelling mind is a danger the Hidden fear almost as much as iron – they're so old and they have so many memories it is only too easy to get lost in the past, to lose hold of reality completely. Perhaps that's what is happening to me. Already.

I sit back on my heels, allowing my gaze to drift upwards and away from the silent waters of the Gateway, relentlessly drawn up the glittering white wall of the cavern till I'm looking right at it: a silver vial no bigger than my hand, resting in a crevice in the rock face fifty metres above my head. The vial contains just a spoonful of my hybrid blood, transfused with a Hidden song of such virulence and power that the contents are enough to spread an unstoppable plague across the face of the earth. An immortal plague.

I'm the only one trapped down here with the power to

open the Gateway – with my mortal blood, I'm immune to the power of the iron magic that seals it – but if I let my father out, he'll release the plague. If my father sees Connie, if he can somehow communicate with her as I just did, a mortal girl immune to the touch of iron, he'll use her to get out of here.

Why did no one think to warn Connie not to meddle? They must have lied to her about me. About what happened. If I put a foot wrong now they will all die: Mum, Nick, Rafe, Dad – even Joe, never mind his stupid bravery and all that *honour*. It will not matter. He'll rot just the same along with the rest of them once my father's plague spreads. And it won't just be my family, either. *Everyone will die.* They'll all pay with their lives for the death of Larkspur's mother so long ago: every single last man, woman and child on earth. He loved her so much.

Oh, Connie. I must tell her the truth, I must stop her—

"Lissy?"

I turn to face the intruder, cold with terror.

It's Iris, not the Swan King, thank God, just mad Iris, and she's standing right behind me, a crown of ivy tangled in her dark hair, her pale face still beautiful even though her mind is broken, shattered into pieces by the terrible punishment my father exacted on her three hundred years ago. It might only be Iris, but how can I have let down my guard in such a foolish way? She might have been standing behind me for ages. What did she see?

"What are you doing here? This is a royal chamber, Iris." I do my best to sound stern and imperious, hoping to scare her away, praying that she didn't spot Connie's image in the waters of the Gateway.

But Iris doesn't cringe, and neither does she run away, back past the guards who have waited outside the White Hall for millennia. Odd how they let her in, but I've no time to worry about that now.

Iris just crouches down beside me, her dark, silvery eyes meeting mine without hesitation. "Lissy," she says, again. "Who was that girl in the water?"

The quartz cavern floor beneath me falls away, and I'm tumbling through empty space. Iris reaches out, placing one white cold hand on my arm, and her touch is so cold it brings me back to the present, and I cannot help shivering. "Lissy, what are you doing?" Iris goes on, urgent and afraid. Justifiably. "Who is that girl? It's not safe to communicate with the mortals, you know. The Swan King will find a way to punish you. He'll find a way to hurt you."

All I can do is stare at her in shocked, silent horror. *She saw.* She saw Connie. Iris starts to shiver, wrapping her slender arms around her body, fingers digging into the silver-white silken dress that clings to her ribcage: Iris is so *fleshless*, even for one of the Hidden. Her eyes seem to lose their focus, as if she is not really looking at me any more, but at something – or someone – else that I can't see. She's losing her hold on the present, falling through cracks in time, back through the centuries to the day her hybrid baby died.

"You need to be careful, Lissy. He punished me – the Swan King punished me," Iris goes on, skeletal fingers now digging into the spare flesh of her arms. "*You led Tippy to the*

White Hall so that she might escape us, he said to me, and his voice was so cold, so terrible, Lissy. *You betrayed me, Iris of the Raven Hair. If you love the mortals so dearly, take a mortal knight for yourself and lie with him till you bear him a half-breed child, and if you die lying with a mortal knight then so be it, and if your child dies, then so be it."*

I take her cold hands in mine, trying to rub in some warmth, to bring Iris back to the present. "You did what was right, Iris. You were the only one who dared to help Tippy. It was wrong of Rose to steal her, wasn't it? To bring her down here? She was just a little girl, missing her mother, her father."

"My baby," Iris whispers. "I couldn't keep him alive—" Her eyes are wild and unfocused.

"*Listen.* What my father did was unforgivable. He should never have punished you the way he did, forcing you to bear a hybrid baby when he knew that it would most likely die. But it's not your fault that he *did* die, Iris."

All I know is that because Iris tried to save Tippy, she's the only one of the Hidden I have any interest in. Having Iris as my only true friend amongst the Hidden is lonely enough, but the rest of them sicken me – too afraid of their king to help a terrified, desperate child.

And God, I can't bear to think of Tippy and how she sacrificed herself to release me and Joe from the Halls of the Hidden. How it was all for nothing, because the Swan King always wins in the end. "Iris—" I reach out, resting one hand on her freezing-cold shoulder, trying to bring her back to now, but her mind is lost in time, and her face is wet with tears.

"And the one I loved, the Hidden boy, he never forgave my betrayal of him – lying with a mortal knight. He was so angry," she whispers. I can't even count the number of times she has told me this tale. "I bore the half-breed child as I was ordered to do. I held my little baby till he died in my arms, and still my love would not forgive me. Oh, Lissy, I lost him, and my baby, everything, with no one to comfort me. I think the Swan King knew what would happen, how I would suffer. Don't let him do the same to you. He will find a way to make you suffer." She looks up at me, her beautiful face bone-white. "There were only two, ever, in the world that we knew about. Only two. Why not my baby?"

I've no idea what she's talking about now – *Only two? Two that we knew about?* "Iris," I say, firmly, "please listen. It's really important you don't tell anyone about the mortal girl you saw me looking at, the girl in the Gateway. Never mind what dreadful punishment he might dream up, if the Swan King sees her there, he will try and contact her, use her to open the Gateway and get out of here. And you know what he'll do then – the plague. You'll never have a chance then to find another mortal knight, to have another hybrid child of your own." All I can rely on is Iris's hatred of my father and her desperate longing for another baby to hold, one who might live. She's said before now that my very existence gives her hope.

Iris stares up at me with a swift, sudden movement that reminds me of a hunting cat. She has returned from the past; she is back in the present. "Of course I won't say anything, Lissy. But you're playing a very dangerous game. You must remember that he will show no mercy if he believes you have wronged him. No mercy at all."

I nod, slowly. It is always so disconcerting the way a conversation with Iris veers through time. Her broken mind skids from century to century. "I know. Listen, I don't have any control over when she comes. All I can do is warn her to stay away—"

"You don't know why I came, do you?" Iris interrupts. She might be my only friend amongst the Hidden, but it really is impossible to hold the course of a conversation with her. I would give a lot just to *talk* to someone again, someone not my father.

Perhaps that is why, in my true heart, I was glad to see Connie's image in the waters of the Gateway, to hear her voice again. I'm lonely. And if I am lonely after six years amongst the Hidden, how will I feel after six hundred? Perhaps I'll forget about Tippy one day, or forget that she mattered. Perhaps I'll dance and sing with the rest of my father's tribe, not caring that for three hundred years they did nothing to help an abandoned child.

"Why are you here, then?" I'm grateful that Iris has lost interest in Connie, for now at least. It *is* unusual to see her in the White Hall – she's so afraid of my father, after all. It must have taken all her courage to come here looking for me, but she just smiles like it's Christmas morning, and it is heartbreaking to see because this is the real Iris again, who she was before my father punished her and broke her mind: a bright, smiling, beautiful Hidden girl and, not for the first time, I wonder who her Hidden lover was – the boy who never forgave Iris for having the baby of a mortal knight. In six long years, I've never managed to hold track of a conversation long enough to make her tell me. "Lissy," Iris says. "Lissy, I've found a corpse."

I swallow, all questions forgotten, desperate to ignore the chilly sensation spreading across my back, between my shoulder blades. Her eyes glitter with hard, bright excitement, and still she smiles.

"A mortal corpse." Iris reaches out and takes both my hands, and God, she's so cold, all the Hidden are so, so cold. "Just bones, Lissy, but the bones reek of iron." She smiles at me, her teeth shining. "Iron. You could kill him, Lissy. You could kill the Swan King. That would solve everything, would it not? Even if your sister opens the Gateway, how could the Swan King release the plague if he was dead and gone?"

9

Larkspur

"Well?" says Nicolas, watching me beneath the desert night. "What in Hell's name does it mean? Who is she?"

"It's Connie Harker." I can't shift my eyes from her image. Gradually, ripples appear from nowhere and spread until she is gone, and all I'm looking at is an iron pot full of dirty water. "It's Lissy's sister. She's the one I healed when Rose gave her a Hidden sickness."

"You *healed* a mortal girl of a Hidden curse?" Nicolas glances across at me, one dark eyebrow delicately arched, and then at the glistening surface of the water. "It looks like that's not all you did."

"Insolent wretch. She's Tainted, wedded to the Hidden world – she's able to pass between the two places in spirit when she sleeps. When she dreams." I frown at the black, glistening water in the pot. "My father told me about Taintings a long time ago but I've never actually seen it before. Connie must be bright-blooded, as your own mother likely was. It's probably why Miriam was able to bear Lissy, why neither of you died. Somewhere in Connie and Lissy's mortal family, there's a line of bright blood, I'm sure of it. When I healed

Connie, she *changed,* her blood set alight. Now she's older, her link to the Hidden is growing even stronger."

"What does that mean, anyway, *bright-blooded*?" Nicolas runs his fingers through his dark hair, raking it back from his face. Unhooded, he never seems to feel the cold as I do.

"The bright-blooded mortals are more akin to the Hidden than the rest of their kind, that's all – less like water and oil than the others." I shrug. "That's why your mothers weren't destroyed bearing half-Hidden children. Why you and Lissy survived as hybrid babies when no others did – or none that we know of. Maybe there are more somewhere, hiding in forgotten corners of the earth." I look away, out at the silvery sand spreading away from us beneath the night; I can't quite bear to meet his eyes. "Remember Iris?" It's hard to say her name: the hollow sourness of my desperation seems to rise again: how I loved her, and how she left me at my father's orders when he punished her for trying to release Tippy. Iris never even looked my way when I was exiled amongst my own kind, when he forbade all the Hidden from even speaking to me. My father broke her. He broke the one I loved, and if I hadn't been such an arrogant fool and shown Iris some mercy when she needed it most – if I had forgiven her for bearing that half-breed child – perhaps she might one day have been mended. Perhaps she might have shown me mercy, too.

Nicolas gives me one of his long looks, half smiling. "How could I forget Iris? I took an arrow in the chest for you the morning you murdered her mortal knight. As I recall, his liegemen had no intention of allowing his death to go

59

unpunished. It's not something I'll forget. It hurt."

"I did not ask you to take that arrow, Nicolas." I hold his gaze. "My father would likely have been more pleased if you'd let me have it."

"Don't be a fool," Nicolas says, quietly. "Anyhow – Lissy Harker is cursed just as surely as I am." When I first told Nicolas about Lissy I thought he'd be pleased he wasn't alone, that he won't be the only person left on earth after the last mortal has withered and died, when the last of the Hidden has been struck down and killed by iron. I was wrong. He frowns. "It makes sense, given what happened to Iris and all the others who tried to bear mortal children – the lovers they chose weren't bright-blooded and the babies didn't survive." He turns to look at me. "What does this Connie girl *want*? Why do I keep seeing her?"

"You know how it is to grieve – more than any man on earth, Nicolas. Connie wants her sister. She wants Lissy. She misses her so much she's drawn closer to the Hidden every time she falls asleep. Each and every one of us, Nicolas, including our brethren still imprisoned with Lissy in the Halls."

"You mean this Connie girl doesn't *know*?" Nicolas whispers, furious. "She has no idea of the danger? What if Connie appears to the Swan King? He'll ask her to open the Gateway."

"Why do you think I'm here? We must act, Nicolas."

"Act *how*?" he demands, hot-headed as ever. "I didn't betray your father and leave him a prisoner of the mortals just so some idiot of a girl could let him out. Dear God,

60

Larkspur, if you only knew how many times in the last three hundred years I've dreamed of him begging me to release you all." He curses, looking away into the fire. "If I hadn't been so sure the Fontevrault would slaughter every last one of you, do you really think I'd have kept the Gateway locked when I had the power to open it?"

"Hush. Have all those centuries not been long enough to cool your temper? Keep your voice down, Nico." I glance at the tents spreading out behind us, but no one stirs. "My father's never going to listen. He won't be stopped. Connie could open the Gateway any moment now. I'm starting to fear there's only one way of ending this."

He frowns, murderous as ever. "Before you ask, I'm not doing it. I'm not going to kill your father."

I sigh, seeing the Swan King at the back of my mind once more, the white feathers of his cloak so pale against his black hair, the cold rage in his eyes as he banished me for the second and final time. *You will never be by my side, child, always away.* I'll hear those words in my mind till my last day on earth, till the day an iron blade finds me at last. I hate him. I hate his cold cruelty and the ruthlessness that keeps the Hidden race imprisoned in the Halls, the mortals too afraid to grant our freedom. A cold ball of misery sits heavily inside my belly. I hate my father but I love him beyond words. I don't want him to die, and yet I can't see another way of ending this. He'll never change his mind. Even if he did, the Fontevrault would never believe he was no danger. They don't trust us, and we will never trust them.

"If Connie lets my father out and he releases the plague, do you really think the Fontevrault will just allow it to happen? Don't be a fool, Nicolas. You're right, the Fontevrault don't need any encouragement to attack the Hidden. If my father has his way, they'll destroy us one by one till we're nothing but a memory, just as they destroyed my mother. There'll be no one to even remember us except you and Lissy. All the mortals will be dead too. I'm afraid that the Fontevrault will only leave us alone if he *is* dead, and no threat to them. Save Lissy, you're the only one who can kill him."

I can't believe those words left my lips. *You're the only one who can kill him.* My father.

Nicolas mutters a curse. "Unless your father's plague destroys the Fontevrault first, before they have a chance to retaliate. Knowing him, it's probably rather potent. In that case, the Hidden will have the earth to themselves once more."

"Are you willing to take that risk?"

"I'm not going to do it, Larkspur. I'm not going to kill him. You know what I owe your father: he gave me a life worth living. What's wrong, are you hungry for the Swan Throne after all these centuries of waiting for it?"

I'm on my feet in a second, hauling him up to face me. "I don't want the throne. I've never wanted that and you know it."

"*Let go of me.*" Nicolas takes my wrists in his hands, but I'm still a little stronger than he is and we stand locked together, holding on to each other. He lets out a long breath, controlling his anger, a feat that I can scarcely help but be impressed by, but even so, I don't let him go. "Look, I'm sorry," he says at last. "I know you don't want the damned throne. What you want is for him to forgive you. Isn't it?"

"He never will, and I can't see another way." If I had not wept every tear I had years ago, I would be weeping now. "As long as my father lives, so does the risk he might release the plague."

"You should have let the girl die and you know it," Nicolas says, his voice harsh. "If she hadn't become Tainted we wouldn't be in this damned mess now. What if she's appeared to your father already? He'll use her to get out of the Halls. Jesus Christ, did you *look* at her, Larkspur? A girl that age, with a face like that? When she sees the Swan King, she's going to think he's all her idiotic dreams come true – without a clue that he's actually her worst nightmare. She'll do anything he asks. Mary, Mother of God, Larkspur – you should have known better. *You should have let her die.*"

I let him go, turning away. He's right. "She was just a little girl when I saved her. Only eight years old. Mortal lives are short enough as it is."

Nicolas gives me one of his narrow-eyed looks, and whispers another curse in a native tongue that no one else even speaks any more. "You're exasperating, Larkspur – do you know that?"

I sigh. "You'd have done the same and saved her if you could. Don't try and tell me otherwise."

He stares into the fire again. "Why are you so sure? I've killed more mortals than I can count." I know he never forgets their faces, though. Still staring at the guttering flames, he speaks again: "I'll kill her too if you ask me. But I

63

won't kill him. Not your father; I owe him too much."

"Connie's just a girl. She doesn't deserve to die. None of this is her fault. We'll have to find another way."

"Like what? The girl – she's *connected* to all of us, Larkspur. If you see her and I see her it's a fool's bet we're the only ones. And if your father persuades her to open the Gateway and he escapes the Halls we both know the cost: not just the mortals' lives but his and all the Hidden. We've held stalemate long enough. It can't go on, not now it's come to this – she's blown it all wide open. There'll be a fight, a bloody fight."

"No one's warned Connie," I say, quietly. "Her family must have lied to her about everything. You know what mortals are like: they conceal the truth. I'm going to warn her, tell her to stop meddling. We might be able to keep this under control ourselves. We just need to reach her before she does anything stupid. Before she makes contact with my father."

Nicolas looks at me from the tail of one dark eye, still facing the campfire. He smiles. "What? It's you and I who will stop this?" And then he laughs, bitter and so tired. "God! Would that there were someone to wish us luck."

I wish more than anything that we could go north together, Nicolas and I, just like that long-ago time when we went everywhere, always together. But I need to be where the mortal world meets the Halls of the Hidden: I need to be at Hopesay Reach. I'll have to go on the wing, and I'll have to go now. "Follow me, Nico."

Nicolas reaches out and we clasp hands, his fingers twined about mine for a heartbeat in the moment before I transform and climb up into the sky in my falcon-form. It would be fruitless to try counting how many times I have wished that flight was not just the gift of the Hidden with royal blood, but that all of my people could fly, safe from mortal arrows and knives, for if that had been true, then my mother would have flown free of her mortal attackers all those centuries ago, and my father would not be what he is now: ruined by the need for revenge. Broken just as surely as Iris. I rise and rise, warm desert air beneath my wings, looking down on my hearth-brother below, standing now to watch me go, the dark robe blowing back from his face. Nicolas is alone once more, just as he has always been.

He is right. It's all about to blow open, wide open, wide as the sky.

10

Connie

I was totally asleep when the Hopesay bus groaned to a halt outside school, shaken awake by the shuddering of the ancient brakes as we stopped. For a moment all I could do was sit leaning against the window. *Lissy*. She'd seemed so real last night, when the Dream came. So close. I could still hear the anger in her voice: *You must not pass.*

She's not dead. She's not dead.

I pushed the thought away. *Lissy's alive. Somewhere. They're just hiding her. Everyone's hiding her from me. It's all a trick.* It felt like such a cold, dead-weight of a certainty, like the knowledge that one day *I* was going to die. But I'd made the mistake of stepping into territory like this before, and where had that left me? Eighteen months of counselling with B.O. Deborah and a lifetime of nervous, wary looks from Mum, like she's waiting for my mind to blow at any moment. And who could blame her?

"Con?" Blue was standing over me, thumbs hooking in the belt loops of his trousers, the familiar tangle of twisted leather bracelets sliding down his wrist. "What's wrong with you? You were completely out of it."

"Thanks a lot for waking me up." I glared at him, elbowing past and knowing I was being vile and unfair, but unable to stop myself. I stumbled down the steps leading off the bus, just so tired I could hardly think straight, let alone successfully place one foot in front of the other.

"Aw, come on, Connie, give me a break!" Blue called, but I ignored him and walked quickly across the scrubby, tired grass, wrapping Mum's huge Indian scarf around my neck and shoulders. I felt so cold and so, so tired, and the last thing I wanted was to be followed, not even by my best friend. I was starting to seriously regret our plans for that night, anyway. Was it really such a great idea to have half the local population under twenty descending on the woods outside my own house? Either way, I had no way of backing out of it now. Even so, I couldn't shake the sick feeling that I'd made a huge mistake planning the party – that something was going to go very wrong.

We had a supply teacher in maths and I made my way right to the back, ignoring the weird looks Blue and Jessie Mayhew shot at me from the front row as I collapsed onto the chair, hunched over my bag. Why did it feel so heavy? I usually sat next to Blue, but couldn't face being first in the line of fire today, and judging by the look of poison Jessie sent towards me she'd decided to make it pretty clear that I was getting in the way so far as Blue was concerned.

"Connie!" Tia Marshall whispered, far too loudly, from her place three seats away. "Connie, I've managed to get my sister to buy loads of vodka for us. Tonight's going to be so, so amazing—"

"Your *sister*?" I couldn't help snapping. Tia's sister was the biggest blabbermouth for miles around, and she was at sixth form in town. I shut my eyes, despairing. Were we now going to have the entire sixth form college descending on the woods as well as half the school?

"She won't *say* anything, Connie. There's no need to be like that."

"The party is meant to be by invitation only," I hissed down the table. "*My* invitation, Tia."

Ignoring Tia, who was now going on and on relentlessly about how I should have been grateful for the supply of vodka, I opened my exercise book and tried to follow the supply teacher's explanation of quadratic equations. I actually didn't need the explanation – I've always just understood maths the same way some people absorb foreign languages with no obvious effort. *Like Lissy used to.* Tears started and I had to look down. If anyone saw I'd never hear the end of it. I stared down at my book and started to work through the examples on the whiteboard. I could hear Kyle Ayrshire and a couple of his mates giving the supply teacher hell, pretending they didn't speak English, but I didn't care. Numbers and letters aligned, all in perfect balance, and my pencil scratched confidently against the paper. Numbers always made me feel peaceful, which I knew also made me a geek of epic proportions, despite my reputation. I still couldn't get Lissy out of my mind, though, sitting with her at the kitchen table doing my maths homework when I was eight years old, and Lissy saying, *You're better at this than I am, Con-con.*

Let me out. Oh, please. The Voice cut straight through my

memories, as if I could hear someone speaking inside my own head. *I've been in darkness so long. I'm lost, Connie. Lost at the Reach—*

His voice. *The* Voice.

And now I wasn't even asleep but hunched over a desk at the back while a supply teacher attempted to ignore the idiots in my class as she droned on about quadratics. And yet I could still hear *him*. The Voice. The hidden boy.

My dreams were leaking through into the real world. Again.

Stop it, I told myself furiously. *You're overtired, Connie. Imagining things.*

I fixed my gaze on the list of equations on the board but I couldn't balance them. For the first time in my life, I couldn't make sense of the numbers.

He's here. Somewhere. He's here.

I leafed back through my exercise book instead, painstakingly tracing the way I'd worked out the last few equations, but even my own handwriting was just a meaningless muddle, numbers and letters drifting across the page like the time I'd smoked a tiny bit of spliff with Amy and Blue and then tried to read my book once I got home. My fingers shook uncontrollably like Uncle Miles's used to when he hadn't had a drink. That's all I really remember about him – his shaking hands – and now mine were just the same.

Help me, Connie. Please. There was something more real about the Voice this time, more definite, less blurred around the edges. Like he was much closer now. And now, just on the very edge of my hearing, I sensed a gentle exhalation. Someone *breathing.* The hairs on the back of my neck froze, like grass caught in a winter frost.

And I looked up to find a boy standing right in front of my desk.

There he was, *right there,* looking down at me with a smile like he was desperate to laugh: taller than anyone I'd ever met, wrapped in some kind of crazy cloak of woven white feathers. And that face – all gorgeous hard angles and a mouth to make you want to die and long dark eyelashes – there was something so familiar about it, like I'd seen him somewhere before, known him in another life, another place. For a second, all I could hear was blood pounding in my ears.

He was so, so beautiful.

He smiled again. *Connie.* His lips didn't move but I heard him calling my name, and I knew his voice. I'd heard it so many times before.

It's him. The boy from the Dream.

Now for the first time I could actually see him. I sat, staring and helpless as a freezing chill spread through my body, holding me rigid in my seat. I couldn't move and I couldn't speak – all I could be certain of was that I was the only person in the room who knew this was happening. Tia Marshall was sitting just three seats away, staring straight through him. The supply teacher didn't even glance our way.

"What do you want?" I whispered. "Who are you?"

I've had so many names. He smiled, so achingly and ridiculously gorgeous. *I need your help, Connie. You'll help me, won't you? I'm trapped, so close to the Reach. I've been a prisoner for such a long time.*

All I could do was stare, silent and helpless. He wasn't real. No one else could see him. This wasn't really happening. But at the same time, he was right in front of me, the feathers of his white cloak rippling faintly in a breeze snaking in through a window the supply teacher had jammed open with an old textbook.

He smiled again and I couldn't breathe; I wanted to reach out and brush one finger down the side of his face, crook it behind his ear, feel those black curls of hair in my hands. Oh, God. How could no one else hear my heart drumming, blood racing through my veins?

I know I can trust you, he said, so gentle and yet so desperate. *All you need to do is move one of the crosses, Connie. One of those iron crosses.*

He was talking about the Reach. About the freaky old crucifixes Mum insisted on leaving nailed above every window and every door. Those silly fairy stories. But he was real – the boy was real. And *trapped*.

Just one. He reached out as if to touch my face. *Just one iron cross, Connie. Please.*

I opened my mouth, still not knowing how to reply, but before I could speak the headache hit me. Everything went white, then black. I couldn't see him any more: he was gone, just gone, my beautiful boy. I'd lost him – just at the moment I'd finally seen his face. How could I help if I couldn't find him? I'd never felt so desperate, so helpless. My head pounded and I swallowed wave after wave of nausea, and only the fear of throwing up in front of our entire maths class gave me the strength to more or less keep my cool.

"Connie Harker?"

I looked up. The supply teacher was right in front of my desk, exactly where the boy had been standing. She looked pissed off, like she'd had enough for the day already and it was only half past nine.

"Get up," she said, obviously thinking that I'd been taking her for a ride just like Kyle and the others.

I'm losing it. I couldn't move. *Hearing voices. Seeing people who aren't really there.* The headache pulsed behind my eyes, relentless.

"Oh, leave her alone, Miss – she's tired. Up all night." Kyle, of course, sleazy as ever, giving the whole class a smug grin, enjoying the chorus of catcalls. I'd fix him later.

To her credit, the supply ignored Kyle completely, clearly made of tougher stuff than most. "I said, get up."

I wanted to tell her I was feeling sick, that my head was pounding, but all I could think about was the black-haired boy who'd been standing in her place just seconds before, his cloak of pure white feathers. It didn't make sense. How could I see someone who wasn't really there? And with such bizarre clothes – that cloak, those feathers – it was just like something from a fairy tale. I hauled myself to my feet, holding on to the desk. Swaying like a drunk.

The supply teacher gave me a very weird look. "Listen, young lady. If you're tired enough to fall asleep in my class, I suggest you explain the reason why to your head of year. I believe Mrs Anderson is in her office now."

More catcalls from Kyle and some of the other more retarded members of the class. The supply teacher ignored them and so did I. My head throbbed, pounding and pounding till I wanted to scream or curl up into a ball in the dark or both. Didn't she realize that if I moved another inch I was going to throw up?

"Con, are you OK?" Blue sounded like he was a thousand miles away instead of sitting just two rows ahead. "Miss, she looks really, really—"

And I never heard the end of Blue's sentence, because waves of darkness just rose and rose until I couldn't see the classroom any more, and all the voices faded, even *his*, and I didn't even feel the pain as my head hit the floor, which Blue told me later it did, with a horrible crack like a dropped egg.

The sickbay reeked of antiseptic and B.O., which really wasn't helping my intense need to vomit. I leaned back in the chair, closing my eyes. The upholstery stank of stale cigarettes, obviously dating from the days when it wasn't completely illegal for teachers to smoke in the staffroom. Even at my school, I doubted that anyone had ever had the cheek to light up in the sickbay. I'd given Mrs Anderson Joe's mobile number, and now all I could do was wait. I'd pretty much managed to fend off most of her questions. Unlike the nurse, who blatantly suspected me of being hungover, and just handed me a photocopied sheet of paper about the possible signs of concussion, Mrs Anderson had seemed genuinely worried. It made a change considering usually all she ever did was tell me what a terrible disappointment I was. *I don't want to see your abilities wasted, Connie. That's the biggest tragedy here.* I was tired of listening to it.

"Connie. What the bloody crap is going on?"

Definitely not Mrs Anderson. I opened my eyes, squinting into the light: Joe, wearing his ragged old jeans and a cashmere jumper Mum had given him three years ago that was now full of holes. He sounded just the same as always, but I couldn't bring myself to look at him let alone answer. "Come on," he said, impatient. "Let's get out of here before they ask either of us any more questions."

He just stood there waiting as I got to my feet, trying to ignore the urge to puke up my guts all over the sickbay floor.

"Take care, Connie," said Mrs Anderson, appearing behind Joe in the doorway. She'd pushed her specs back into her frizzy grey hair, her face taut with worry. "Please do keep a good eye on her, Joe. It's really not like Connie to faint and if she shows any signs of concussion, straight to A&E, OK? She's never usually ill, are you?" She raised one eyebrow, a trick I'd always wished I could master. "Never off school unless we have one of those unfortunate incidents like last term."

At any other time I would have said, *When you suspended me, you mean?* But I felt too ill to risk it. Mrs Anderson was always giving me crap, but I knew that at least she liked me, which was one of the two reasons I hadn't been permanently excluded: that and the fact that my exam results were predicted to single-handedly propel the school right up the league tables. Not that I'd be taking any GCSEs at this school if Dad got his way.

"Right," Joe said, which judging from his tone was Yorkshire for *fuck off*.

"What am I going to do about the exam? It's meant to be this afternoon. My dad's going to kill me if I don't take it."

Mrs Anderson raised her eyebrows. "I'm sure we can rearrange the entrance exam." She gave me a funny little half smile. "To be frank, Connie, we don't want to lose a girl of your intelligence, but I'm perfectly happy to explain matters to your father and to the school if need be. I really do think I should call your mother, though."

My chest constricted. I knew Dad wouldn't listen to Mrs Anderson: he was far too arrogant to take a teacher seriously, and so far as he was concerned, I was starting at Lissy's old school in September, like it or not. It was a foregone conclusion that I'd pass the entrance exam. "Please don't call Mum. She'll only worry. The funeral's tomorrow and she'll never be able to get back to the airport in time to catch a flight, anyway." I couldn't stand thinking of Mum arriving home just in time to discover half the teenage population in a hundred-mile radius congregating in the woods behind the Reach. That would put a rocket underneath her if nothing else would. Maybe then at least she'd finally show some interest. How far had news of the party spread? I'd forbidden anyone to mention it on Facebook, on pain of death, but it would only take one comment for the whole thing to go up like an atomic mushroom cloud.

Joe stood silently, just waiting. There was something about him that made you not want to mess. Even Mrs Anderson seemed to pick up on it, and she could face a classroom mutiny without even flinching. She glanced at him briefly, as if appraising his suitability as a chaperone one final time, then nodded. "OK, Connie. We'll see you on Monday. Take it easy over the weekend, won't you?" She gave me one of those awful searching looks – her speciality – and I realized she'd heard rumours about the party, guessing I was at the centre of it all, even if no one had told her as much. *Please don't say anything*, I prayed – not that Joe was likely to care, anyway – but Mrs Anderson just held the door open for us, and gave me another long, hard look before saying, "Take care, Connie, won't you?"

I followed Joe out to the van without a word and he slid into the driver's seat beside me, moving with bored, lazy grace. His battered old jeans were ripped at the knee, and when he reached for the steering wheel the worn-out cuff of his jumper grazed the back of his hand. He smelled faintly of washing powder and something else I couldn't quite put my finger on.

"What's wrong?" Joe asked, not even looking at me as he pulled out of the school car park. I'd been totally called out for staring at him. Red heat spread up my chest, an embarrassing and incriminating blush blooming right across my face.

"Nothing." *Stop staring at your stepbrother, Connie. It's really not cool. You've already made a move on him while drunk. This is not a good development.*

In the back of my mind I heard Amy laugh, saying, *Guys are like buses, Con. You spend ages waiting, thinking you'll be alone for the rest of your life, and then they all come along at once.*

Right. Except that I was obsessing over one boy who was a complete figment of my imagination, with a cloak of woven white feathers, and blatantly ogling another who happened to be my stepbrother, and who incidentally was also six years older than me and still in love with my dead sister.

You're a loser of epic proportions, Connie Harker. Telling myself as much didn't help.

Keeping his eyes on the road, Joe changed gear. His hands were tanned from working outside, dusted with fine golden hairs. "No, I mean what happened at school? Why did you pass out?"

Oh, God. Was it actually possible to go any redder? I looked down at the Tippex stain on my navy school skirt. "I don't know. I fainted, I suppose. Nothing Mum needs to know about, OK? I'm on special report already." Being a juvenile delinquent was actually kind of embarrassing now I was sitting there in the van with Joe. I didn't feel like some kind of cool rebel then. I felt small and stupid.

He laughed, then, for the first time. "Why?"

I was almost too humiliated to tell him. "We went on a school trip and I took a bottle of whisky. This girl got really ill, Lucy Bentley. It was bad. She got in tons of trouble with her parents, and I was suspended. Seriously, Joe, Mum really doesn't need to know about today. She was close to not going to this funeral, but she's named as an executor of the will and I'm supposed to be sitting the entrance exam for – for boarding school." I couldn't bring myself to say *Lissy's old school*. I gazed out of the window. "My dad's going to go crazy when he finds out I got sent home instead. "He's convinced himself that going away to some prison camp will make me less of a screw-up."

Joe pulled over into a lay-by to let a tractor past, his eyes fixed on the narrow lane ahead. "Right. Throwing some money at the problem."

"I'm a *problem*?" Was that really how everyone saw me? A pain in the neck, like a broken boiler.

Joe laughed. "Come on, of course you're a problem. You're a bloody nutter." He hauled the van out into the road again. "You look rough," he went on. "Maybe just get some rest."

I shook my head. "I really don't want to go to sleep. I really don't." And the words were out before I had time to reconsider: "Joe, I keep having these bizarre dreams. All the time. It's scaring me, OK? Seriously." I stopped short of telling him about the boy. He was my secret. Just for me.

Joe shot me a funny look then, like he was sizing me up. "Don't be daft. You do look really knackered and stressed. No wonder you're having weird dreams. Don't worry about this exam thing. You passed out in school – it's not like you did it on purpose. Your dad can't exactly blame you for that."

"No way, he's gong to think I did it on purpose to get out of the exam. He knows I don't want to change schools." I squeezed my eyes shut. There wasn't a whole lot Dad could do to me – Elena wouldn't allow me to cross the threshold of their fancy apartment in London, and Mum knew that it was pointless to try grounding me when I could just let myself out of the house in the middle of the night. But even so, Dad in a rage was always horrendous. It was the way he didn't even raise his voice. The way he was so *disappointed*.

"Don't worry about it, Con. What can he do?"

I wondered if that was just Joe's way of telling me he didn't want to know. The headache was getting worse every moment and I leaned back in the seat, resting my head against the window. Why had I even thought that he would in any way understand? How could he? I was obviously just doomed to make a complete idiot of myself every time I saw him. I should have cut my losses and shut up. Suddenly, I just couldn't shake the need to talk about it. To talk about my sister with someone else who'd actually known her, even though mentioning her name to Joe would always be a mistake.

He fell in love with Lissy, Rafe had told me. *He took it really hard when she died.*

"It's Lissy." I turned my head, pretending not to look at him. The first time I'd spoken her name in six years, and it was like spitting out a stone, cold and alien. "I keep dreaming about Lissy." I'd done it – I'd finally said her name, and it felt like jumping off a huge rock, tumbling to the sea far below.

Joe flinched – a muscle in his jaw jumped and twitched. "Well, then, you're a bloody idiot. She's not coming back, Connie."

A kind of ragged, burning fury overtook me then. "I didn't say she was coming back, did I? She's dead, Joe. I know she's dead, OK? Forget I ever said anything."

She's not coming back? What a weird thing to say. Even I wasn't stupid enough to believe that death isn't the end.

"Maybe just shut up, Connie, and stop going on about what you don't understand? Lissy died. Deal with it."

I turned to him, bright hot anger welling up. "Jesus, how dare you? It's not my fault I've been dreaming about her, OK? She was my sister. I just wanted to talk to someone. Forget I even said anything." There was more I was longing to say but although I could have slapped him, I needed Joe onside. The last thing I wanted was for Mum to come running back to Hopesay early only to find I'd planned a mini festival in her absence. I turned my pounding head to one side so I was looking out of the window instead of at Joe, at his hand on the gearstick, the way he hadn't shaved for a few days, the distracting smell of washing powder and that other indefinable faint scent, diesel and something else I couldn't place. Infuriating.

Please. You've got to help me. Move the crosses, Connie—

The Voice. Again.

I shivered, tearing my gaze away from the hedgerows flashing past the van window to glance back at Joe, who was still staring at the road ahead like nothing had happened. He hadn't heard. *I was the only one.* OK, so Mum had always told me that if we got rid of the iron crucifixes from the Reach, no one from the village would ever set foot in the house again – but all that stuff was just a load of stupid old fairy stories. None of those old stories were really true. How could they be?

I had to let go of Lissy. *She's not coming back.* Obsessing over her was really starting to mess with my head. I'd hallucinated in a maths class, now I was hearing a voice from my dreams in broad daylight. What if I was seriously, genuinely ill just like everyone used to think? Like, mentally ill?

All right, there's one way to prove whether all this is just your mind playing tricks on you, Connie Harker. Only one way to prove whether or not you've lost your grip on reality.

All I needed to do was wait till we got home, which wouldn't take long judging by the way my disconcertingly attractive stepbrother was driving. Wait till we got home and move the first crucifix I could lay my hands on. What harm could it do, really? Of course nothing would happen, but at least then I'd know if I was sick in the head. Maybe it was time to get some help. And every time I closed my eyes, I saw the boy's face: his hair blacker than coal, the cloak of white feathers and his smile – his beautiful secret smile, just for me.

I couldn't deny that a part of me wanted him to be real.

11

Lissy

It is black in the lost tunnels of the Hidden – just deep and endless black, dark nothing. Iris knows her way without light, and I have no argument with that – the less likely we are to be spotted by anyone else, the better. Treason. We're planning treason. *Murder*. The air here is moist and rank – centuries of damp leaching out of ancient bedrock. Wet gravelly soil scrunches unpleasantly beneath my bare feet. I sense Iris's presence just ahead of me – the darkness is without end down here, but I can hear the gentle rhythm of her breathing, her footfalls just a few paces ahead of mine. I can't help listening out, just waiting to be caught.

At last, Iris stops. "Just here. Wait."

Relief washes over me, rapidly replaced by fear. There's no sickly sweet smell of decomposition. I'd feared something rotten, but that's obviously all over now. But what if it's Dad? Rafe? Or even Joe? What if one of them did try to follow me after all? Judging by the way Connie has aged I must have been down here for almost six years. Long enough for a corpse to become nothing but bones.

"We need to see," I whisper, urgent and panicking, and I

blow on my palm till the warmth of my breath coalesces into a globe of silver light.

"I can't go any closer." Iris gasps, as if she's trying not to be sick. She flattens herself against the nearest wall, holding one hand up to cover her mouth. "Can't you smell it, Lissy? The iron?"

What has my life become? A prisoner scurrying around in the dark, my only friend a Hidden girl with a broken mind; the pair of us planning a murder? My heart races and I squat down, my gown trailing in the damp, sticking to my legs. Shadows leap, but the skeleton is easy enough to see – lying face down, one arm reaching out, strands of wiry grey hair still plastered to the skull. Not Rafe then. Or Dad. They were both blond last time I saw them, but perhaps years of wandering alone in the darkness would be enough to strip the colour from anyone's hair. Tears spring to my eyes, trailing down my face. What must it be like to die down here, so desperate and alone? I know I've got to take a closer look, to know for sure who this was. I reach out, reluctantly brushing my fingers against a wizened strip of fabric still stuck to the ribcage. It looks as if it has been nibbled by mice. Or rats. Another wave of cold horror rolls over me. I take the fabric between thumb and forefinger, tugging gently. Silent, it comes away from the bones and I hold it up to the globe of light resting in my other palm.

It's tweed. Stained green tweed.

I know that jacket. I saw it, years ago, hanging in the boot room at Hopesay Reach. I never met the owner, but I know who he was. Who I hope he was – anyone can take a coat, after all.

"It's Miles Conway," I whisper.

Iris draws in a deep, shuddering breath. It's always horrible to see the effect iron has on the Hidden. How they can't even bear to be near it.

"Miles," she whispers. "He's the one who opened the Gateway last time. Twenty years ago – Rose's lover, her mortal knight."

I look down at the stained, rag-draped bones. *Miles*. It really could be him. He must have died searching for Rose. Miles grew up with legends of the Hidden – stories of so much power that he couldn't resist finding out if they were true. Miles and Rose. Mum and the Swan King. They were both so young. So completely and utterly stupid and naive. *Oh, Mum*. I'm never going to see her again: there's no breaking a Hidden bargain, and I came to the Halls with my father to save Connie's life. She's cursed. If I leave, she'll die. Even if I wait down here for years and years – the entire length of Connie's life – by the time I walk out into the daylight again, Connie and most likely everyone else I know will be dead and gone. Mum, Dad, Rafe. Joe. All gone. The world will have moved on without me, and I'll be a stranger to everybody. Even then, the Swan King will still have my blood – how could I ever be sure he wouldn't release the plague?

Unless he were dead?

"Maybe Miles came looking for Rose," I say, quietly. "How awful. And it was all for nothing: he had no chance of finding her." I'll never forget the moment Joe killed Rose, flinging that iron knife into her face as she tried to stop us escaping back into the mortal world through the Western Caverns, her cry as she lay dying. We thought we were free. We thought we'd won. We couldn't have been more wrong. My father always wins. Every time.

"I don't care, Lissy!" Iris hisses. "Just search him and find the iron – *please*. I can't stand it for much longer."

"I don't think we should be here. What do you want me to do, Iris? Kill my father? Is that what you're asking me to do?"

Iris stares at me, cowering against the damp earthen tunnel wall, as far away from the stench of iron as she can get. "Please, Lissy."

Mum. All this started with her. Had she really loved him, the Swan King? Would she forgive me? I stare at Iris. "Listen. Just say that I did kill the King, that I murdered my own father… Would that mean the bargain was broken? That the curse on my sister would just dissolve into nothing?"

Iris nods, slowly. "In the moment of his death, your sister will be free of the curse. You could leave here and Connie would live. Think about it, Lissy. With the Swan King dead, the rest of us would be free to negotiate with the Fontevrault again. *He's* the one keeping us down here – it's their fear he'll release the plague."

She's right. In a twisted way, killing the Swan King really would solve everything. There will be no danger of the plague being released once he's dead. It's just that I can't forget the change in him when I said, *Honour her memory with love*. As if, finally, he might be giving up on the idea of revenge. It would solve everything, but I'd be a murderer.

Killing is always wrong, isn't it? *Taking a life.*

I lean over the skeleton, searching for what's left of Miles's other hand. My fingertips brush over damp bone and I can't stop shivering, but now I'm touching something else – cold, smooth and hard. "It's some kind of metal tube." I sit back on my heels, lifting it up. All I can hear is the hollow clatter of tiny radial bones against the raw bedrock and Iris's rapid, shallow breathing. It's a rifle. I'm touching the barrel of a gun, and it's heavy.

"It's a mortal weapon, isn't it?" Iris whispers, her voice harsh – so desperate. "Can you use it, Lissy?"

If Miles had a gun, he must also have come with ammunition. The gun's too heavy for me to hold one-handed. I blow the globe of light away from my fingertips so that it hovers unaided in the air above his bones and take the rifle in both hands, running my fingers down the stained and rusted barrel till I find the safety catch beneath. I squeeze it, holding my breath. It doesn't move, rusted solid.

"It's ruined." And the truth is, I'm relieved. Because in that tiny second before Iris arrived in the White Hall, I'd got through to my father. I know I had. I am so sure of it. I could see the change in his eyes when I spoke of Larkspur's mother. *Don't honour her memory with blood. Honour it with love.*

"There must be something you can do with it," Iris hisses, her voice so brittle and tense I can tell she hasn't got long. We can't stay much longer.

I sit back on my heels. "I'm sorry, Iris – but to actually kill one of the Hidden the iron has to enter your bloodstream, doesn't it? This is a rifle, not a blade. It's completely ruined –

I can't fire it, even if I could find any bullets."

Iris lets out a sigh. "I'm afraid, Lissy. So afraid."

Me too. "We should get back to the White Hall. The last thing we need is for him to suspect us of treason. We've been gone long enough. You know how he is – he always notices everything."

I look up, away from the mortal remains of Miles – I've been squatting in the same position for too long, and I reach back to lean on one hand. My palm rests against cold metal, and I freeze. *Iron. More iron.* Miles wasn't just carrying his rifle but something else, too. I shift my weight and my fingers slowly close around the small, blunt-ended iron shape lying amongst the damp shingle. It's mine now. Turning, I uncurl my fingers and show Iris the knife, the pitted, corroded blade – just a dull glimmer in my silver light.

"I'm afraid to use it, Iris. It's wrong. Killing is wrong, no matter what he's done – what he *wants* to do. What he's guilty of."

"I'm afraid, too." Iris looks up, fixing her gaze on me. "But I'm more afraid about that little mortal girl in the waters of the Gateway. What if he uses her to get out, and the Fontevrault come searching for the Hidden, hunting the Swan King? They're mortal – the iron magic in the Reach won't stop them. They could come through the Gateway any time they liked, swarming through the tunnels like rats, stalking down each and every one of us. All your father needs to do is give the Fontevrault a reason to attack, and they will."

She hasn't forgotten, then.

"Lissy," Iris hisses, "if the mortals are meddling with the Gateway again, just as Miles did twenty years ago, then we're far too close to danger. Far too close. The Hidden long for their freedom but we can't risk the Gateway being opened whilst your father still lives." Iris sounds collected and reasonable again – it's so disconcerting, this constant shift between a girl lost in time, a prisoner of her own terrible memories, and Iris's real self, the girl she was before my father broke her mind. "Listen – if the Swan King releases his plague, the Fontevrault will show us no mercy. We'll *all* die." I hear nothing but the panicked and rag-torn rhythm of her breath. "His time is up, Lissy, and you know it. He must die – with the Swan King gone, you'd be free to open the Gateway at last. You'll see your mortal family again and the Fontevrault might show mercy to the rest of us if you can persuade them we mean no harm. There's a chance they might leave us in peace."

We both stare down at the penknife resting in the palm of my hand, Iris recoiling a little. She's right. I have to kill him. I have to be a murderer. Connie won't have a clue. In her eyes, the Swan King is only a wild and beautiful young man, with an otherworldly air that will make her skin crawl, and yet she still won't be able to resist him. She won't be the first mortal to fall for one of the Hidden. I feel so helpless, torn between committing murder or waiting for disaster.

12

Joe

The second I parked the van outside the Reach Connie was off and running down the drive, slamming the passenger door after her. *Thanks a lot, Dad. Cheers, Miriam.* Connie was trouble, pure and simple – I felt like someone had just handed me a live hand grenade with the pin out, ready to blow at any second. Why couldn't they have got someone else to look after her for a week? From what Dad had told me, that uptight bitch Adam had married refused to have Connie in the house, but was his bloody job really so important that he couldn't have come down here, or at least kicked Elena out for a few days? Connie was his kid, not mine.

It was obvious that neither of her parents gave that much of a crap about what happened to her. It was all about Lissy, everyone all torn up inside with grief. It was no surprise that Connie had turned out a screw-up. She wasn't stupid: she must've known that after Lissy went, her parents just weren't that bothered about anyone else. Which was pretty unnatural, really, from where I was standing. Connie was still their kid, after all. But she'd just blamed herself. And all that about dreams and Lissy. A wave of sick fear rolled over me.

Everyone had lied to Connie about Lissy, protecting her from the Fontevrault. But wouldn't it have been better – safer – if she'd known the truth?

I slumped in my seat, watching my liability of a stepsister shove open the huge, arched front door, blonde hair spilling down the back of her navy school jumper. The door swung shut behind her and I was left alone, just sitting in the van on the drive outside the Reach. How long was it since I'd been here? Six years at least. Dad and I never really talked about this unspoken arrangement. It wasn't that I didn't want to see him. I didn't even mind Miriam. It was just I couldn't believe they'd stayed here. Not after what happened. I intended to die knowing I could count my visits to Hopesay Reach on one hand. It was a bad place.

And it had changed, the Reach. Not the house – that was the same as always: a great sprawling, rambling mess of a place with a hundred glittering windows tucked away in odd corners, and that tangle of red-brick Tudor chimneys on the rooftop. I let my eyes travel up that way, remembering the day Rafe and me had climbed out of the attic window and hidden among the chimney stacks as the Fontevrault searched every inch of the house below, hunting us down because we knew too much about the Hidden. The gardens had been tidied, though – that overgrown lawn mown into a smooth green carpet, flower-beds jammed full of colour. It was like being at a proper stately home, the kind Mam dragged me to as a kid.

Lissy's here. So close, but so far away. Trapped.

I looked away from the gardens and back to the Reach

itself, watching the huge old front door − ancient wood bleached almost white by the sun − till I could be sure Connie had gone inside and wasn't coming back. I climbed out of the van and stood on the driveway, gravel crunching beneath my boots; I knew where I was going, even though it was wrong. Even though it was completely bloody daft. No. Worse than that: stupid. Dangerous and stupid, but I couldn't stop myself. The grass was still wet with dew, staining my boots as I crossed the lawn, closer to the lake with every step. Closer to the Gateway. The reeds and bulrushes had been hacked back and lilies floated on the dark water. It was like some kind of ornamental bloody pond, not the gateway to another world.

What would happen if I just walked right in? Found myself in that white, glittering cave again, just like years ago? Would Lissy be there still or was she lost somewhere in those endless black tunnels? How were the Hidden treating her? Was she kept as a prisoner? I remembered running into the water after her as she went with the Swan King, Rafe and Adam holding me back, the sheer desperation of it. How could they do that? How could they just let her go? None of this was her fault. Lissy in exchange for Connie's life, that's what the Swan King had demanded, no doubt convinced that once he'd got Lissy on his side of the Gateway, he'd be able to convince her to open it. He hadn't so far, but Christ only knew what lengths of persuasion he'd gone to, what she'd been made to suffer. And in exchange for Lissy's freedom, we'd got Connie and Rafe, for what they were worth. Adam had been forced to choose between his children − to let

Connie and Rafe die or Lissy go as a prisoner. I couldn't help wondering if he ever regretted that choice, given that Connie had turned out pretty much nothing but a royal pain in the arse, and Rafe hadn't been home in years.

Deep cold travelled up my legs and I shivered, wrapping both arms around myself. My feet were wet. I looked down, and I was ankle-deep, walking into the waters of the Gateway without even thinking straight. Just thinking about Lissy. It would be so easy to cross over, no danger to anyone else but me. I shuddered with sudden cold, and a wind blew up out of nowhere, shaking the branches of the old yew tree. What harm would it do, really, if I carried on going, walking into the water till I found myself in that other world? If I just crossed over into the Halls of the Hidden only to see how Lissy was doing, if she was treated OK? If I knew that she wasn't being harmed, I might be able to forget her, just a little bit. Find some nice girl, have a normal life instead of hiding up on the fell with Grandad. *If, if, if, bloody if.*

But you don't want a nice girl, you daft bugger. You want her. You want Lissy.

I knew that was the real truth of it. I wanted Lissy; I never even knew if she wanted me. Wanting her was enough. For the thousandth time, I asked myself what difference would it make to anyone if I just disappeared into the Halls and was never seen again? I was a pretty crushing disappointment to Mam and Dad as it was. Maybe it'd be better if I just went for good. At least I'd be with her. Otherwise I'd be like bloody Miles Conway the rest of my life, pining after a Hidden girl

I'd never, ever be able to forget, just like the way he was when he got old and saggy and Rose lost interest. What'd happened to him down there? He'd followed Lissy and the Swan King through the Gateway, looking for Rose. Not that he'd find her. I'd made sure of that.

The cold intensified and I looked down to see water lapping around my knees. Just a few steps further. That's all it would take, and then that rushing, rushing of grey water past my eyes, opening them again to find myself in the White Hall, my clothes dry as a bone. I was so close. Within reach—

But there was Connie to think of.

She was just a kid, even if she was bloody annoying, and she had no one else looking out for her, no one except me. I couldn't leave her alone. It hurt so much to walk away, though; every step took me further from Lissy, and I'd been so close to seeing her again. *So close.* Mud sucked at the heels of my boots, and when I reached the lakeshore I was on my knees in thick, algae-stained muck, unable just for that moment in time to take another step, spent and hollow. I put a hand to my face to push away my hair and the skin was wet with tears.

Lissy was out of reach, just like always, and I couldn't even see for the tears, crying just like a little kid. Blurry-eyed, I forced myself up onto my feet and walked back across the lawn to the house. It looked so innocent and warm, sprawling on the lawn, June sunshine glancing off the windows, ancient stone glowing gold in the morning light. *Goddamned place should have been burned to the ground years ago and then we wouldn't be in this mess.* And I could have done it then.

I swear I would have struck a kitchen match and laid it against the dusty old curtains, just watching them light up. I would have gone with them, too. Not even looking back, I'd have burned myself to the bone.

13

Lissy

In the darkness of the Halls, I run my finger along the edge of the metal object in my hand, feeling a small ridge running almost along its entire length. Miles's penknife, now forced shut. I tuck it into the wide silk belt of my gown, a rigid little thing digging into my side. A steel blade. Steel is made of iron. I'll never get another opportunity like this to kill the Swan King – there'd be no more threat of plague, of mass-murder on an unimaginable scale. The Hidden will be free. I'll see Mum again. Dad. Connie. I'll breathe fresh air again and see the sky. My family. My old life. But do I really need to be a killer? The Swan King has changed his mind, I'd swear on the lives of all my mortal family. He's given up the idea of revenge at last – at long, long last.

Don't honour her memory with blood. Honour it with love.

I follow Iris along the tunnel, leaving Miles's bones to their long and lonely eternity in the forgotten reaches of the Halls. Iris is right: I have to kill him. I can't take the chance that he might use Connie to open the Gateway. I'm going to be a killer whether I like it or not: I have no choice.

14

Joe

The front hallway was cool and dark as ever, a single stream of dusty light pouring in through the tiny window. I could hear a steady pattering as my clothes dripped onto the flagstones. What was Connie going to think when she saw the state I was in? All I could do was hope she'd shut herself in her room, looking at some crap on her phone or writing emo poetry – whatever it was girls like her did when they were pissed off with the universe – although knowing Connie she was probably just smoking a fag out of the nearest window.

It was lighter in the kitchen when I came down in dry clothes. There was something different about it but I couldn't put my finger on what. Still the same enormous black stove in the fireplace, but the old wooden table was now covered with a bright cloth, there were flowery curtains and boxes of cereal lined up on top of the fridge, a bottle of washing-up liquid stood by the sink and a new radio was plugged in next to the kettle – all signs that normal life had been resumed at the Reach now that Miles had disappeared after living here feral for all those years. I shuddered thinking about him, scavenging the woods for birds like a fox, those dusty half-empty bottles of champagne in the fridge, and the way he'd followed Lissy down into the Halls like that, searching for Rose. He'd be looking a long time. Murderers are supposed to feel guilty but if I had my time again I'd still kill Rose. I didn't regret it, and I knew that made me a broken man, that there had to be something missing in my head to feel like that after taking a life, but I didn't care. She deserved it.

I pulled back a chair and slumped at the table, wishing I had the energy to make coffee. A five-hour drive and now this. Even after so many years Lissy still had so much power over me. Just being that close to the possibility of seeing her drained me bloodless, just to nothing.

The Reach was quiet – all I could hear was the faint gurgling of water in the knackered old radiators, the ticking of the kitchen clock. Still no sign of Connie. The door to the back hallway was open, just a crack. Had she gone out that way? Out towards the woods? A faint chill of fear passed through me, and looking down I saw goosebumps rise on my forearms.

Bloody Connie.

I knew without even thinking about it that I'd have to go after her. I'd learned a long time ago never to question an instinct like that. I got up, shoving back my chair, and that was when I looked up at the kitchen window and realized it wasn't just the new curtains that made everything look so different. So wrong.

Six years before, on that desperate morning we closed the Gateway, I'd nailed an iron cross to the lintel above the kitchen window. Now it was gone, leaving only a pale silhouette behind to show where it had once been. A cross, taken: someone had opened the Gateway again. And even though I knew it meant that the Swan King's plague was coming, and the end of everything, all I could think of was Lissy, and whether I would see her one last time before I died.

15

Lissy

Just steps away from the entrance to the White Hall I hear a light, metallic clink. The guards have crossed their spears, blocking my path. Behind me, I hear the hurried rhythm of Iris's breathing. She's afraid, just as much as I am. The guards smell the iron just as she did. I knew it would come to this. They're hooded, waiting. I never even knew their names; I hardly ever see their faces. They're so ancient, older than my father by a long way, young when seas of lava boiled where London is now, before continents broke apart and began their long slow migration across the face of the earth. And they know I am carrying iron.

"Let me by."

A long, slow hiss of laughter. When one of the guards speaks, her voice is thin and dry like dead grass blown across a desert. "What game are you playing, half-blood child?"

"I'm not playing."

"You come armed. You carry iron into the Halls of the King. You shall not pass." They both step away, unable to bear the iron-scent emanating from my clothes, rising from the knife pressing against my body.

I thrust my hand into the folds of my gown and withdraw the knife, tugging it free from my belt, and both guards recoil, hissing, their ancient faces hidden by their hooded cloaks. "Will you lay down your lives for him?" I ask, quietly. "Are you sure? His time has come and gone."

And the guards, I realize now, have seen Hidden kings and queens come and go before – so many, many times. For a new king to rise up, another must fall. They have done this before, been in this place before. The moment of silence stretches on and on and then, without a single word, they step back, away from me, letting their spears drop, clattering against the ground.

They betray him without hesitation: the choice is made.

"Courage, Lissy," Iris whispers, but I don't need her now. My father's guards have betrayed him. It's over already. This is between me and my father. Leaving her, I walk alone into the White Hall and thank God he is alone, kneeling at the water's edge, the cloak of white feathers tumbling out behind him, so pale against his black hair.

All I can hear is the soft hiss of his breathing, so gentle, and my heartbeat hammering away in my ears. I grip the knife's handle – smooth plastic. He knows I'm here and he can surely sense the iron, but he doesn't move; he doesn't even make a sound. *Keep going.* I cross the White Hall and it seems to take for ever, and still he doesn't look round; he's completely focused on the Gateway, on the water. I glance up at the cavern wall, and the silver vial is still there, wedged safely into a crack in the rock face. And yet this doesn't mean much – what did he say to me?

Your blood is not so very hard to come by, daughter.

And in a rush, those words come back to me: *Don't honour her memory with blood. Honour it with love.* I was so sure he was on the brink of change, giving up the idea of revenge. Isn't there just a chance – a tiny chance – that my father and I might step into the dark waters of the Gateway side by side, that we might be free together and with no blood spilt; his long dreams of plague and death and revenge all over, all gone?

Honour her memory with love.

I kneel at his side and he still doesn't look at me. Iris is right. Even if my father has given up on the idea of revenge, the Fontevrault would never believe it. In their eyes, he'll always be a danger. I'm holding the knife and he knows I have it. Of course he does. He looks up at last and glancing down at the knife in my hand, he gives me a faint smile, completely unafraid. A cool trickle of fear slides down my back. What does this mean? God only knows how much self-control it must take for him not to recoil from the scent of the iron as Iris and the guards did.

I lay the blade between us on the quartz floor of the cavern, saying nothing. It's always so bright in here compared with the rest of the Halls; the light hurts my eyes, glancing off the silver steel, the incongruous blue plastic handle. My father looks down at it, smiling, then at me.

"I don't want to use it." My stomach churns. "Truly, I don't."

"Really?" He looks at me with such yearning.

"You've seen Connie – my sister. I know you have."

He never takes his eyes away from mine, like he's absorbing

101

every last detail of my face. "What did you expect, Lissy —
that your family would just let you go? She is your sister.
Your blood kin. You are bound to one another. Of course
she came looking for you, whether she meant to or not, even
if it was only in her dreams. And Connie's dreams are not
those of other mortals. She *travels*, Lissy. She's not an ordinary
mortal girl."

Oh, God. What's happened to her?

It's what he has been waiting for all this time. I might have
refused to open the Gateway, but I could do nothing about
this. *Oh, Connie.* The knife waits on the ground between us.
Beyond the White Hall, I hear Iris's voice rising with panic
— more Hidden voices raised in anger. A scream — a struggle?
Are the guards actually keeping the rest of the Hidden out,
those willing to fight for their king? The air in the Halls of
the Hidden is thick with betrayal on this day, but how deep
does the treason run?

My father seems to pay no attention to the noise outside.
"It's all right, Lissy," he says. "I know. My time as King of
the Hidden has slipped away like so many grains of sand.
The Fontevrault know too well that I would do anything
to annihilate the mortal race; I've done nothing but ensure
the imprisonment of my people." He smiles at the gathering
voices outside the White Hall, voices raised in anger, in victory.
"But more to the point, Lissy, it seems that the Hidden do not
share my desire for revenge. It seems that the Hidden cannot
wait for ever to be free."

"It doesn't have to be like that," I say.

It's as if he hasn't even heard me. "I couldn't help it,

daughter," he whispers. "I just missed her so much, and I was so, so angry."

Tears slide down my face. "Don't—"

"Lissy." He smiles at me. "Look."

As one, we both turn to the Gateway, and as I watch a change moves across the face of the black and glittering waters. The darkness fades to grey then deep, endless blue trailed with drifts of cloud. It's the sky. We're actually looking at the sky above the Reach. Now I see more detail – the shadow of a tree, leaves shifting in a wind I can't feel down here. It's the way out, and it's open.

Freedom. It's the sky. I never thought I'd see the sky again.

"You did it. You persuaded Connie to open the Gateway." I speak in a dry whisper, throat desiccated with fear.

"She's so lovely," he says, simply. "So like your mother. Golden and warm – so very warm. I would give a lot just to hold one more mortal girl in my arms, Lissy."

"Not that one." I won't let him touch her. Won't let him near her. My eyes travel back to the Gateway – it's a window now, just for the Hidden. They are free at last, the iron magic dissolved once more. A window to a lost world. The sky is so blue that it hurts my eyes: it's hard to absorb all that colour after so many endless years down here in the darkness of the Halls. My father smiles, and as one, we both turn away from the Gateway, from the brightness of the sky, and we look up at the crystalline quartz wall above it all. The silver vial still sits untouched, resting on a thin ledge far above my head. My blood. If he'd really wanted to release the plague, he would have done it by now.

Surely?

"Do you know the mortals say we have no souls?" my father asks, gently. "We may not share the agony of their short lives, but once dead, the Hidden are truly gone, snuffed out like candle flames."

"No one really knows what happens when we die, mortal or not." My voice is shaking. "No one has ever returned to tell us."

He smiles. "Do you think, then, that there is a chance I might see her again? My own love?"

I can't answer that, but his desperation chills me. "We could walk out of here together, you and I. We could negotiate with the Fontevrault and be free."

"Lissy, my dear child, if you learn one thing from me, it must be never to negotiate with the Fontevrault. If I hadn't done that, Larkspur's mother would still be at my side, and they would not have cut her throat with an iron knife in the forest beyond Fontevrault Abbey." He smiles once more, desolate. "My time is over, daughter. Listen to them calling for my blood. The Hidden want their freedom, and all I want is darkness if I cannot have her. Only you can grant their freedom, Lissy. Only you."

"No—" I hiss. *What is he asking me to do?*

"What I would really like," my father whispers, "is to see Larkspur one last time. If I called them now, Lissy, will they come, do you think?" His voice breaks a little on those last few words.

Them? What does he mean by that? He's confused, making mistakes.

"You know that Larkspur will come. But it doesn't have to be for one last time."

He hasn't taken my blood, not yet, but the sky is so blue, so open and so free. Is he actually inviting me to take his life – begging me to, even? And yet the Swan King has outwitted me before. In the end he always wins. Doesn't he? I look up into his face, and all I see in his eyes is grief, endless grief and a desperate longing that can never be salved. But with my father, there's always a catch. Always. I watch my hand move; I snatch the knife so fast, but he could still stop me if he chose. He can move quicker than I can. But he doesn't. We're so close, kneeling within arm's reach of one another.

"You too?" he says, his voice so soft and gentle. "You would betray me? Really, Lissy?"

"You asked me to do it."

The Gateway is open. He's tricked me before. I can't take the risk. My hand flies out, fisted around the plastic handle of the knife. He doesn't move; he only waits. I stop, fist poised in mid-air. I let the knife fall into my lap, useless.

"I can't do it." I sound so *normal*.

And then my father says, "*Please*."

I stare at him. *What?*

"*The guards let you in*, Lissy. It is done. Please."

He's been betrayed so many times. He's alone. I'm all he has.

And I can't trust him.

My hand rises. The plastic knife handle is slippery, the palm of my hand folded around it, fingers gripping, slipping. The blade is small and pitted with corrosion. It's nothing but a cheap penknife, and it's just me and him. We sit so close our knees are almost touching, the feathers of his cloak falling into my lap as if an enormous pillow has burst between us; the most beautiful and lonely and desperate and evil creature I have ever known. My father. He wanted me so much that he changed the world to get me.

And I cut him. I reach out and I cut him. I draw a thin blue line of blood down the side of my father's face with the very sharpest tip of the penknife, and all the time he does nothing but watch me. He doesn't so much as flinch, even though the pain and horror of the iron must be worse than anything I can imagine.

"I'm sorry—" The words fly out in a whisper, a gasp.

All I hear is the softest exhalation. "*Ah*—" And in his eyes I see the real truth. He would not have released the plague. I could have granted my father his freedom, only he no longer wanted it. I reach out and take his hands in mine.

"I can't see her," he whispers. "I still can't see her. Oh, is that you, my own love? Please let it be you." He reaches out for me, my father, and I hold on to him. In the moment of his dying, has he mistaken me for Larkspur's mother? Or does he see something that I can't, that I'll never see because I can't die?

"It's me," I whisper, anything to bring him comfort, cradling his dark head against my shoulder, and my father sobs with relief. In the moment of his death he is warm to the touch just like any beautiful mortal boy, only now I'm holding on to nothing, just nothing, and all I can see are white feathers, spinning furiously in the air, filling the White

Hall, catching in my hair, drifting into my mouth, blinding me, and all I hear is the ragged sound of my own sobbing, because in the end nothing could save him. I killed him. I killed my father, the last to betray him. He's gone. The Swan King is dead.

The feathers fall so silently and when they hit the quartz floor they become as nothing, just nothing. All is quiet, and when at last I look up, half blind with tears, I see the Hidden gathering, filing into the White Hall in complete silence, watching me and waiting, so beautiful in their ragged clothes. Iris leads them. It's she who speaks, she with the crown of ivy in her hair, and I wonder if she was chosen in secret by the rest of the Hidden to engineer this, to steer me along the path I've taken, knowing that Iris was the only one I trusted, because she was the only one in the Halls who had tried to help Tippy. How deep did the betrayal of my father truly run?

I'm a murderer. I killed him. For all the dreadful things he did, he was my father, and he was desperate, alone till the last.

"Hail the Hawk Queen," Iris says, so gently, so sweet, and there's a light in her eyes I've never seen before. She's so close to what she wants. What she so urgently needs. A baby, a child to hold in her arms at last. What have I done?

I stand: I turn to face them. "You're free, but I can't be your queen. The throne is Larkspur's right, not mine. And now at last he can return to us." It's a struggle to keep my voice steady. I'm a murderer. I killed my own father.

They all wait, still silent, for *Iris* to speak. How long has this been planned? Did they all betray him? Every last one of the Hidden?

Iris smiles. "But Lissy, Larkspur is not here. Larkspur is not the one who killed his father."

"What do you mean?" I hear blood pounding in my ears. I want to go home. The Hidden can't stop me going home now. I stand up, ready to step into the waters of the Gateway, to walk out onto the lawn at Hopesay Reach. Will Mum be there? Rafe? Connie?

Mum. I thought I'd never see her again—

"Larkspur was born a misfit," Iris goes on. "He was born with too much mercy, Lissy. It's why he betrayed your father. It's why he took you home to your mother when you were a baby, and why he was exiled. It's why he didn't allow your little sister to die of the Hidden sickness Rose touched her with. He should have let her die, Lissy, shouldn't he? But he couldn't. Do you really think we would choose a creature of Larkspur's stamp to be our king? Even his own father knew he could never rule."

I stare at her, horrified. She had me fooled so easily: she wasn't acting alone. She never had been.

I step closer to the water, and when I speak my voice shakes with rage and shock. "Well, choose a new ruler from your own number, then, Iris, because I never swore to be your queen. I'm going home. I've waited long enough to see my family again."

The Hidden watch without a single word. I can feel their eyes on me, though. All watching, all waiting as one by one the drift of white feathers surrounding me fades into nothing.

There is now nothing left of my father at all, and a burning sensation spreads across my back and between my shoulders as the last of those white feathers fades into nothing and disappears. It's as if I'm shape-changing into my hawk-form without actually intending to, with no control over it at all.

Stop! I scream at myself, but the burning across my shoulders only gets worse and all I can see is the Hidden watching me, so calm and impassive, and Iris standing before all of them, like this is what she has been waiting for all along.

"You have no choice, Lissy," she says, smiling gently. "You took the king's life. You are now the Hawk Queen whether you choose it or not."

And the burning spreads over my entire body, only I'm not shape-changing, I'm screaming. I can't stop screaming because this is something different, something new. And I see feathers whirling again in the White Hall, but this time they are not the snow-pale of a swan, but honey-golden and tawny-brown. They are the feathers of a hawk, and the White Hall is full of my screaming, because I see what Iris was planning, what she and the rest of the Hidden wanted all along. Agony tears through my body, and I rise to my feet, facing her. Iris wanted a Hawk Queen to lead her out beneath the mortal sky so she could bear another hybrid baby, one that might live this time, and the Hidden want to leave the Halls for ever. They chose her to lead their deception, knowing she was the only one of their number I even half trusted, all because she was the only one, apart from Larkspur himself, who tried to save poor Tippy, the only one of the Hidden who tried to release a poor, lonely mortal child from the Halls— A dense weight gathers at my shoulders, soft warmth encompassing my bare arms, the cool weight of a silver clasp at my throat.

Iris tricked me – they all did. This is what they wanted. I'm nothing but the key to their freedom. I look down and wish I had not, because all I see is golden-brown feathers. I am now wrapped in a cloak all my own: I am the Hawk Queen. I'm what the Hidden wanted. Horror boils up inside me – Iris used me, she tricked me and now I've changed, I've become *something else*— The pain recedes and I can speak again. The Gateway is open before me with the wide-open sky just a step away, and Hawk Queen or not, I'm going home.

"Let us out, Hawk Queen. Let us feel the wind in our hair, O Queen." Hundreds of voices rise up as one. "Lead us to freedom. We'll follow you. We'll follow you, dear Hawk Queen."

I turn to them. I don't want to rule the Hidden. They tricked me and I hate every single last one of them. "If the Fontevrault come to Hopesay now, they'll kill you all."

"They won't find us, Lissy." So many voices, all making the same plea. "We'll be so quiet, Lissy. So still. We just want to breathe clean air. We all need clean air, Lissy."

And as one, before I can do anything to stop them, the Hidden begin to move forwards towards the Gateway, towards the open blue sky.

16

Nicolas de Mercadier

I leave the car parked in the market square. The hire company are expecting it to arrive in London tomorrow but what are they going to do about it? Kill me? I don't even find this funny any more.

I'm following A-roads rather than motorways in case the Fontevrault have somehow picked up my trail already. I've been here before – it's just another rainswept English town – but the last time I came was centuries ago. The town square used to be filled with rats and ragged children begging for scraps, but now it's lined with neat little cafes, tables and chairs sheltered from the unseasonal rain by bright umbrellas branded with the logos of those who peddle beer and cigarettes, both of which I could kill for at this moment but haven't got time to find.

Larkspur needs me.

He needs me: the Swan King. He saved my mother's life, all those hundreds of years ago when they struck the covenant at Fontevrault, and even though she's been dust for centuries, the debt still holds. If the Swan King gets out, the Fontevrault will kill him, even now. They'll hunt him down, and all I can do is pray to a God I'll never meet that Larkspur will get to the Reach in time to intervene.

I don't trust this half-mortal girl – *Lissy*. She's too young, still mortal enough to miss the family she left behind, miss them so much that she'd do anything – anything – to see them again. I should know. After all Anjou did to me when I was a child, I was still the one with him when he died alone in that battlefield tent. He was King Henry of England then, but abandoned by all his own sons and daughters, and God, I've lost so many that I mourn those I hated almost as much as I mourn those I loved. Mortals feel so deeply for their kin. Memories crowd in again, overwhelming me with their force and colour – so many faces, whispered voices, all gone, all dust, all nothing. At the back of my mind three hundred years have tumbled away into darkness as if they never were and I'm not here any more, not sitting by this fountain in this busy little English town square, but kneeling before the Swan King in the White Hall, on the morning I chose to leave, the morning I saved Larkspur's life; the morning he killed Iris's mortal lover with a single arrow, and we were hunted—

The White Hall is utterly silent. Even the wild sound of Iris's sobbing has faded; she's been led away, her half-mortal baby now cold in the ground. Which leaves just Larkspur and me – and his father.

I would rather be anywhere else on earth than here. My bloodsoaked shirt clings to my chest, but no matter how much I bleed, whether that mortal arrow pierced a lung or even my heart, I can't die. It hurts, though. An unending ache.

The Swan King does not even look at Larkspur. "Nicolas," he

112

says to me gently, "you took an arrow meant for my son. A worthless life, I will allow — but Hidden all the same. What is your price for saving it?"

"Make peace with your son." I glance at Larkspur. He looks straight ahead, as if he can neither hear nor see us.

"How can there be peace when he plots against me?" the Swan King replies. "Now, what will you have? What can I offer? He might be worthless, but he is my kin. I ought to give you something."

"No," Larkspur says, quietly. "Don't say that. All we did — all we tried to do was help Tippy. She's just a little girl. She wants to go home. Iris and I —" he breaks off, helpless with grief — "we didn't deserve — this."

"Silence!" His father raps out the order in a tone of such violence that Larkspur actually takes a step back.

"I will not be silent!" Larkspur's voice fills the White Hall. "You destroyed Iris. You gave her to a mortal knight, her child died and now her mind is broken. You took her away from me, all because we disobeyed you. What did you expect me to do?"

The Swan King only smiles at him. "Did I order you to turn Iris away when she took her mortal lover? Did I command you to send her from your side as the half-breed child grew in her womb? No. That was your own jealousy, child. You made your own punishment. Did I even order you to kill the mortal knight? No. Nicolas is a more loyal son to me than my own child."

As long as I am here, they will never be at peace, and that's the bitter truth.

Larkspur speaks in a furious whisper. "You made Iris suffer just because we tried to send Tippy home to her mother. You broke Iris's mind, just for that—"

"Be quiet, both of you!" I can't stand it any more. Cold fear shudders through me — have I really just ordered the Swan King into silence? But I can't bear this any longer, the battle between these two. Nothing is ever forgiven, and nothing forgotten. I wonder if forgiveness is a mortal blessing. When you know that one day you'll both be dead and gone, letting go of a quarrel makes more sense.

"What have you to say, then, Nicolas?" The Swan King's voice is so soft, almost gentle, but I know him well enough to be sure he is now almost as angry with me as he is with Larkspur.

"I will go." I keep my voice steady. I want no part in this damnable endless battle, this constant sparring. I only make it worse between them. If I were not here, the Swan King would have no favourite. For nearly six hundred years I've lived amongst the Hidden and these walls are closing in on me. It's time to go.

"Nicolas, don't," Larkspur whispers.

The Swan King ignores him, just staring at me, not a hair changed from the day he found me broken and bleeding by the walls of Fontevrault. "Are you certain, Nicolas? Everyone you love in the mortal world will die. You will watch them all die."

I nod. "It's time." We use no titles down here; never once have I called him sire or my lord. He's been more of a father to me than I've ever had.

He reaches out, taking my hand in his, and God, his touch is so, so cold. "The mortal world is a dangerous place for you now, Nicolas. Never stay in one place long enough for them to see you cannot grow old, or the Fontevrault will find you. Nicolas, they will hunt you down. Don't spend eternity in their cells, my child. Don't let them use you as a weapon, either. In the mortal world, *these are dangers you must face. Is it what you want?"*

"I want to see the leaves fall in autumn. I want to see frost on a spider's web." I look up at him. I want to say, too, that as long as I stay, Larkspur will never be good enough for him. That's only the truth. And it's not right. If I go, there's a chance they might one day have peace. "I owe you all – everything," I say. "I can't repay it."

I still remember waking, broken and bleeding, at the foot of the abbey wall at Fontevrault, the easy command in his voice as he ordered me to stand, then just as quickly bade me run.

The Swan King smiles. "Go then, Nicolas de Mercadier."

I nod, not daring to speak. He is wild and cruel, but I would do anything for him.

I turn to Larkspur. He has lost everything: Iris, his father's love. And now I'm about to go, too. We are like brothers, and I'm leaving him. "You know they are dead now, Nicolas?" he says. "Your mother? All your kin? Even their children?"

"I know."

There's no place for me here. It is only the Swan King and Larkspur. I step forward into the cold, cold waters of the Gateway. It's time to go home, back to the mortal world.

Beside the fountain, I draw in a deep breath, taking control of my mind once more. Too many memories. If I let them wash over me, they'll wash me right away till there's nothing left but an empty shell, and still no way to die, no way for it all to be over. No one to share this with. Even Larkspur will meet the edge of an iron blade one day, but I'll be alone for ever. I listen to the water play; it splashes cool against my fingers as I scoop a handful to drink, so grateful for the cold relief of it. If I keep driving at this rate, I'll be at the Reach in a matter of hours, but is that going to be too late? There's no point in wondering. I've just got to keep going. There's no choice.

I stare around the square, watching all the people sitting beneath the umbrellas despite the rain, eating, drinking and laughing with no idea of the risk. Not one of them has the smallest notion of the danger they're all in – what the Swan King will unleash on the world if this Connie girl is desperate and foolish enough to open the Gateway. They'll all be dead within days; Larkspur told me, and I can believe it. I've seen enough mortal plagues to know how quickly an immortal one will devastate them, and the Swan King has been waiting almost nine hundred years for this. Nothing will stop him: nothing will change his mind.

My throat's still raging hot with thirst and I turn back to the fountain to scoop another handful, but as I look into the pool I don't see the algae-stained white tiles lining the base but feathers, hundreds of feathers, twisting and whirling underwater.

No.

The feathers spin in a white vortex until, gradually, they begin to thin out, to fade away completely, and in the water of the fountain I see an image of a black-haired boy lying on his back, one arm crooked beneath his head as if he's only sleeping, and my heart lurches. It's him, it's the Swan King, but now there is just the faintest of dark blue lines down one side of his face.

Hidden blood.

A cold, wet breeze picks up, swirling through the town square, rippling the water, distorting the image. Even so, I have seen enough, and my heart swells with desperate sorrow.

He's dead.

If you want to save your mother's life, child, then you'd better run. For centuries, the Swan King and Larkspur were all I had, more dear to me than any mortal family. How many times have I dreamed of him begging me to open the Gateway, begging me to release the Hidden? I stare at the fountain, at the image in the water, at the Swan King lying so still as the swirling feathers fade to nothing around him. He looks just the same as ever, so young and beautiful, but he's gone, just gone, and I owe him so much, and it's my fault. If I hadn't refused to open the Gateway after Tippy de Conway's brother had it sealed, if I hadn't ignored the Swan King's cries for mercy, his face in my dreams, century after century, he would not be dead. He would be free.

I only wanted to protect you, save you from an iron blade—

And just as I'm the only one who could have saved the King from that iron knife, there is only one who could have wielded that weapon.

The girl. Larkspur's sister: Lissy Harker.

The Swan King fades before my eyes till I'm only looking at the bottom of the fountain, and white-hot fury sweeps through me with the raging force of a forest fire. She killed him, and he saved me, and I betrayed him. I left the Hidden to their imprisonment, sure that was a better fate than being endlessly hunted through the centuries by the Fontevrault. I was too late to save him. I may not be able to kill Lissy

Harker, but now thanks to Larkspur I know exactly how to make her suffer, how to make her feel sorrow that cuts this deep. The little golden-haired girl is her sister. Connie Harker might be bright-blooded and Tainted, but she's still mortal. She can still die if I choose to make her.

I choose it.

17

Connie

I crashed along the path through the woods, feeling like the world's biggest idiot. I just wanted to get as far from the Reach as I possibly could. Far away from Joe – God, how embarrassing, ogling him like that. And then the way he'd flipped when I mentioned Lissy. Stopping, I hurled the iron cross as hard into the bracken as I could, breathing hard. Nothing had happened when I moved it from the window above the kitchen sink, prising those nails out of the wall with a claw hammer from the DIY drawer. Of course nothing had happened.

What did you expect, you idiot? A beautiful boy in a cloak made of white feathers to suddenly just appear and whisk you off into the sunset?

I'd imagined the whole thing. Everything. He wasn't real. *Obviously*. But he'd seemed so *real* in the classroom, though. Like I could have reached out and touched him. I must have been dreaming or letting my imagination run away with me. Either that or I was losing my mind. How unbelievably lame to have concocted a story like that all by myself – I couldn't stop cringing just thinking about it. Now I was miles away from school and alone in the woods I'd known for years, the Dream seemed far less real. Of course I wasn't going mad. I'd fallen asleep in maths: that was all. It didn't mean anything. It didn't mean that there was something terrible and wrong with my brain. It was a dream, not a hallucination. If I were mad, I'd still believe the boy was real. I wouldn't even be considering the possibility that the whole thing was just a dream.

A boy with a cloak made of white feathers? For Christ's sake, Connie.

And now Joe blatantly thought I was some kind of freak, dreaming about Lissy. He'd been so angry the truth was he'd scared me, just a little. Why didn't he just get over her? Six years had passed. He and Lissy had hardly even known each other when she died, for God's sake. He had no right to miss her so much. She was my sister – she'd never even been his girlfriend and yet he was obsessed. How was I going to face him now? We had to live in the same house for a whole week, and probably the worst thing was that, on top of everything, he knew that I still blatantly thought he was hot. The way I'd stared at him in the car? Oh, God.

You're such a loser, Connie Harker.

I strode on through the woods. It had to be almost lunchtime by now, but the idea of eating anything made my stomach churn. At least I wasn't sitting in geography. At least Mrs Anderson had stopped short of calling Mum and summoning her home from France. I'd almost reached the beech coppice where me and Blue would be helping Amy's boyfriend, Nye, set up his sound system in just a few hours. What was Joe going to make of the party? I pushed on through the bracken, furiously batting the green fronds away from my legs with an old branch.

Which was when I heard the drumming.

I stopped, branch hanging loose by my side. *Drumming?*

Oh, shit. News of the party had clearly spread much further than I'd realized. There were people up in the far woods already – the kind who enjoyed impromptu drum circles. Who, in my experience of tagging along to illegal outdoor parties with Amy, Nye and Blue, were also very often the kind of people who had their own vans, their own generators, a lot of hair and a lot of dogs. They definitely weren't going to listen if I told them that tonight was strictly invitation only.

This was getting way out of control. The drumming was growing louder every second. I could hear singing now, too – a high, clear voice, brighter than the stars on a clear winter night. I couldn't understand a word: it was all in some other language I half recognized, as if from a dream. It sounded almost like hissing. There were far too many "s" sounds. It was completely freaky.

I walked on through the tangle of bracken, trying to be quiet. Even if these guys were pretty much just going to laugh in my face if I asked them to move on, I might still be able to get some kind of an idea how many of them there were. If it looked really bad, I could always tell Blue not to bring the sound system. Without music, even if people from school did turn up, maybe they wouldn't stay long, especially if word got round that we'd cancelled.

Yeah, right, I told myself. *A free house is a free house. Who's going to care if there's music or not? It's not exactly like there's a hundred other entertainment options around here on a Friday night. If there's no music up here, they'll just descend on the Reach instead.*

Oh, God.

I could hear laughter now, too, and people talking – all in that weird hissing language. There was something *familiar* about it, similar to Welsh maybe – we were pretty close to the border. But it wasn't Welsh. I pushed through the last of the trees until the clearing finally opened out before me, filled with shards of sunlight knifing down through the trees – and people. There were *hundreds* of them. Hundreds. For ages, all I could do was stand there, just staring. They were all so tall, so tall and strange and beautiful. They were just like the boy in my Dream. Just like the boy in his cloak of white feathers. He'd begged me to free him, to move just a single iron cross from the Reach.

A wave of hot nausea washed through me. *Connie, what the* hell *have you done?*

Who were these people? They were all so ridiculously gorgeous and yet their clothes were just absolutely ragged – filthy scraps of silk and animal hide. It was like walking into some kind of freaky fashion shoot. They all looked like models. They were exactly like Lissy, I realized – Lissy and the boy from my Dream. She looked just like him – different colouring, but now I knew why he'd seemed so familiar: *he was like Lissy,* their faces echoed each other. Why the hell had I been dreaming about a boy who looked exactly like my

122

dead sister? And now the woods were heaving with people just like both of them.

I left the safety of the trees and walked closer. I couldn't help myself – I was drawn to them all. I just kept putting one foot in front of the other even though every instinct was screaming at me to run. They were dancing, writhing to the beat of the drums, laughing and calling to one another, all so pale and so beautiful. None of them seemed to pay me any attention – it was like I wasn't even there. Before I'd given it any thought at all dancing figures surrounded me completely, lithe as snakes, dirty hair flying out around them. They spun and twisted among the trees, their beautiful faces upturned to the sky, teeth shining as they laughed and sang in their strange language.

And then the nearest ones just stopped, standing dead still and staring at me, all smiling. All boys – but tall, beautiful boys with wild hair and such pale skin it was as if they'd never seen the sun. The one closest to me stepped a little nearer – his hair was the rusty brown of dead bracken in winter, and the buckles on his boots clinked a little as he walked.

"Hello, little girl," he said, and then he laughed. They'd known I was there all along. They'd been playing with me, just like a cat toys with a mouse: they'd let me walk right in among them thinking that no one had noticed.

Idiot, idiot, idiot.

As one, all the boys suddenly seemed a lot closer without me even seeing them move. I could smell the stale, unwashed scent of their clothes, the sweetness of their breath. *Oh, God.*

I wished like crazy that Blue was there to make some sort of dumb remark that would make it all seem like a joke.

"So will you dance with us, Connie?" the rusty-haired boy said, reaching out to let one long, white finger trail down the side of my face, shuddering with pleasure the second his skin came into contact with mine. His touch was so cold that I gasped, and he knew my name. I couldn't move. He'd called me Connie: he knew who I was. I couldn't speak. He took my hands in his, and God, he was just so unbearably cold.

"Such warmth," he whispered, and his beautiful lips parted, letting out a sigh. "Such beauty and such warmth, little girl." It was obvious what he wanted, pulling me towards him, closer with every breath, running his freezing-cold hands all over my body, sliding them up inside my school shirt, his thumbs pressing into my bare belly as he pulled me closer still, so that all I could smell was the stale, musty stink of the ragged skins he wore. It was like I'd been frozen. And it was at the moment he pulled me hard up against his lean body that I realized he wasn't human. There was something alien about him, just too different. Not human, but something else – something with enormous strength and power. Different, like Lissy in my dream, just like Lissy.

Run, I screamed at myself. *You've got to run.*

I screamed, and when my scream died, fading into the branches of the trees above, he was still there, his breath in my face, and a single voice cut through the silence, cold and utterly chilling in its fury.

"*Let her go.*"

I knew that voice. I knew it.

Lissy. It was Lissy. And I knew I had to be already dead, or dreaming, because Lissy was gone and there was no way I'd hear her voice in the waking world ever again. She was gone, she was gone—

"*Now.*" Her voice. Lissy's voice, but so angry—

And the rusty-haired boy was torn away from me by a force I couldn't see, jerked free of my body as if snatched by a giant hand, his eyes wild with rage and fear. I sat up, breathing hard, watching as he flew across the clearing just like a doll hurled by a child having a tantrum, landing hard in the shadows. And the rest of them did nothing but watch in silence. Sobbing, I scrambled to my feet, spinning around. I was surrounded: they had all gathered in a circle around me, silent. Watching. I sensed someone right behind me and whirled back to face them, heart hammering, sweat pouring freely down my back.

I came face to face with a girl. *No, not a girl. Something else.*

She was immensely tall, towering above me, and wrapped in a cloak of golden-brown feathers that swept to the ground all around her, a pool of shining feathers at her feet. A girl with tangled red hair and a face I'd known since the day I was born, because she was the second person in the world to hold me.

"Lissy." I could hardly speak with enormous relief and shock. It was her. Not dead. Living and breathing right in front of me. My sister. But she'd changed. She was different – even more so than she'd been when I saw her in my dreams. Taller, and somehow like a cat that had once been a pet but that was now wild, ruthless and powerful.

She's not dead, she's not dead, she's not dead…

"Connie." Lissy stepped towards me. "Didn't I warn you? Didn't I tell you to stay away? You should never have opened the Gateway. I had to kill him."

What was she talking about? This couldn't be happening. "You're not really here," I whispered. "You can't be here."

She smiled, the anger fading as she reached out to take my hand. "It's really me, Connie. I promise."

We reached out, holding each other so close I could hear the slow beat of her heart as I pressed my head against her chest. She was so tall.

"It can't be you. Oh, Lissy, it can't be you."

She laughed, like we were the only two people in the whole world, not at the centre of a crowd of freakishly tall and beautiful creatures who were all watching us like some kind of street theatre performance. "It's really me, Connie. But you shouldn't have opened the Gateway—"

"You're dead," I whispered, and she let go of me like I was burning her. "You can't be here because you're dead."

And for a second she looked just like the old Lissy again – so vulnerable. "*What?* I'm what?"

They laughed. The rest of the creatures started to laugh, watching and smiling.

"Let us have the little girl, O Queen," one called. "Come on, let us take her. She's so warm and we've been so cold for so long."

"Let us have her, Lissy. You can never go home now. Let us keep her, Lissy – to play with."

She turned to face the crowd in a whirl of golden feathers. "Be quiet!"

"Let us take her. She can never be yours again. Why not let us take her?"

It was clear that Lissy was no longer in control. We were alone. And what the hell had they called her? *Queen?*

"Stay close to me," Lissy whispered, and her face was streaked with tears. "I'll manage this, Connie." Her voice rang out across the clearing. "I didn't ask for this and I never wanted it. Perhaps next time you ought to be more careful what you wish for. If I'm really your ruler, you'll have to learn to obey me." She hardly lifted her voice, but it carried right across the clearing, slicing through the rush of rising chatter. "Leave my sister alone."

On the far side of the group, the rusty-haired boy was standing again, leaning forward, straining against the grip of those who were holding him back. He laughed. "What right have you got to deny us the heat of a mortal girl?" he demanded. "We've waited so long, Lissy. You released us: bear the consequences."

"Do you want to keep your freedom or not, Briar?" Lissy's voice carried effortlessly. "Take yourself another mortal girl if that's what you're so desperate for and see how quickly the Fontevrault come running. We're here to negotiate our freedom. Unless of course you want them to come after you with weapons of iron? Unless you want all the Hidden to be completely wiped out?"

"Lissy?" I hissed. "What are you talking about? What's the Fontevrault?" *The Hidden? Weapons of iron?* None of it made any sense. I felt like I was dreaming again or even hallucinating – this simply just couldn't be the real world, not with my dead sister in it, talking about all these crazy things that made no sense at all.

Lissy turned to me, her bone-white face so alien, somehow. "Listen, Connie. Everything you've ever been told about me? It's a lie."

And that was the first time the truth really sank in. It wasn't what she said, but the dead-white glow to her skin, her height — she wasn't just model-tall now but freakishly tall, cloaked in all those shimmering golden feathers, that dirty silver gown clinging to her legs.

Lissy wasn't dead, but just like those other beautiful creatures, she certainly wasn't human, either.

18

Joe

I sprinted out through the boot room and into the yard, half blind with panic, my vision blurring. Slamming into the fence, I saw fresh boot prints on the muddy lane that twisted away up the hillside, soon hidden by trees. Connie had been running, and the missing crucifix had just disappeared – it wasn't in the kitchen or the hallway or anywhere obvious at all. I couldn't put it back, which meant I had no way of sealing the Gateway. All I could do was find her, quickly. What if the Swan King had already crossed back over into the mortal world? Connie had no idea what she was dealing with, what she had unleashed. Not a clue.

I sprinted up the lane, skidding in the wet mud, yelling her name over and over again, but apart from my own voice, the woods were quiet. I stopped, panting: I knew I had to give myself the chance to listen, to assess the situation. It was the wrong kind of quiet. I couldn't hear any birdsong, no soft shuffling and crackling as small creatures moved through the undergrowth, either. Dead kind of quiet, like you get when the rest of nature knows there's something wrong and runs for it.

I'd heard that kind of silence before. Six years ago, the day I stepped out the back door at Hopesay Reach and saw Connie talking to a young girl with hair as white as snow. *Rose—*

The further into the woods I got, I heard voices, drumming, even. And then it all stopped, just nothing but complete thick silence again. I tore on through the trees, and then all of a sudden there they were, the Hidden, walking all swift and silent towards me with sunlight in their hair, cloaks swirling about their legs. There must have been six or seven at least, weirdly tall and dressed in those scraps of silk, leather and fur, just walking silently towards me between the trees like fish slipping through fronds of seaweed. I stopped, heart pounding. I couldn't look away from their faces: their dark, glittering eyes.

The Hidden only smiled at me, each and every last one of them – like I was the best joke they'd ever seen – and it was only knowing that Connie must have ventured further into the woods that stopped me running like hell in the other direction: I just knew that as a member of team *Homo sapiens* I was in the presence of a higher predator. And as the Hidden smiled, their white teeth glistened, and I couldn't help wondering if the whole death-by-iron thing extended to the haemoglobin in human blood and how hungry the Hidden really were after their incarceration.

Why wasn't I already dead? Why hadn't the plague been released?

Before I had the chance to ask any questions, they all just swept past me. The closest one's heavy woollen cloak brushed my arm, and I almost choked on the stale reek of campfire smoke and unwashed hair.

I stood still for a second, alone on the path once they'd passed, watching them slip away through the trees. Hidden roaming all over the mortal world like sewer-rats, but no plague, or at least I wasn't dead yet. I couldn't make sense of it. Connie's boot prints led off the path and away into the trees, and I ran, passing more Hidden all the time. Some of them paused to give me a disinterested glance, like I was a worm or a fly. Most didn't, and as the trees thinned out it was like the Hidden multiplied even as I was watching – they were all gathered together, crowded around like they were watching something. Or someone. There were so many of them, hundreds and hundreds – I'd lost track of Connie's footprints completely, and I had to push my way between the gathered Hidden, just calling her name.

If the Hidden were here then did that mean Lissy was, too?

Without even thinking about it, I stopped yelling for Connie. "Lissy!" I shouted. "Lissy!"

I stopped. Hidden blocked my path every way I turned. I was surrounded. *Prey.* I'd not seen the Swan King, though. Not yet. They all just stood there, silently watching me, hundreds of pairs of identical gunmetal-grey eyes, each bearing an expression I couldn't read.

"Lissy!" My voice bounced back at me from between the trees.

"*Joe.*"

She spoke from somewhere behind me and I couldn't

move. She sounded different – colder, almost – but I knew it was her; I knew it was Lissy. I'd listened to her whispering my name every night in my dreams since the cold grey dawn she'd walked into the lake at Hopesay Reach, arm in arm with the Swan King. I'd waited six years for this moment and now it had come I was frozen. Slowly, I turned to face her. And then there Lissy was, draped in this huge, feathered cloak, gold and brown and every shade in between, iridescent, shining feathers. She stood with her arm around Connie's shoulders, the feathers of her cloak shivering in the breeze, tangling among her dark red hair. Connie looked white and frightened, just clinging on to her sister, but I couldn't have cared less about Connie at that moment. It was all about Lissy, just like everything had always been about Lissy since the day I saw her standing in that dark lane the night we first came to the Reach.

Lissy was *different*, though, taller and bone-white. *Inhuman.* I stepped closer. "You're all right," I said, like a bloody idiot. "You're OK."

It took everything I had not to actually cry like a little kid. She'd spent every night of the last six years inhabiting my dreams, taking over my mind, and now there we were in front of each other and it was all I could think to say.

Lissy smiled and wild hope flooded through my body. Did she feel like I did? Had she dreamed about me like I'd dreamed about her, sorry to wake up every morning because all that meant was that I had to drag myself through the day without seeing her face? Our fingers twined together and she was so cold, so bloody cold. So Hidden.

"Thank you, Joe," Lissy said, quietly, and she stepped away from Connie, leaving her standing alone, surrounded by Hidden, but at that moment I couldn't think about Connie at all; all I could think of was Lissy. And then it was only me and her, and everyone else all around us just faded to nothing – they didn't even matter. We stood face to face, Lissy's cold white hand in mine. Her eyes glistened with tears. "You tried to follow me into the lake that morning, didn't you? You tried to follow me through the Gateway, but Dad and Rafe stopped you. Thank you for being the only one who tried … for trying to save me."

I reached out for her other hand and she let me take it, just gripping on to each other, hands held in fists right up to our chests, so close that I could have kissed her.

"What else was I meant to do?" And it took all I had not to let go of Lissy's hands and hold her in my arms. "Where is he?" I asked, after what seemed like a thousand years had passed. "Where's your father? Why hasn't this plague thing spread everywhere? Me and your sister ought to be dead by now. Everyone should be. What's going on?"

"He's dead," Lissy said, simply. "I killed him, just like you killed Rose. It was so easy."

I stared at her, waves of elation rolling over me like warm water. The Swan King was dead. *She was free.*

"I killed him," Lissy said again, like she was trying to make herself believe it. "He's dead, Joe."

"So you're really free?" My voice shook like I was about to cry. "Lissy, this is going to sound crazy but I've missed you – just so much." I couldn't go on. I looked up into her face, realizing for the first time that she was now a little taller than me. I remembered the look in her eyes the first evening we met, the way she just didn't seem to care about all the normal boring crap we'd to put up with – exams, idiots at school, all that stuff just didn't seem to carry any weight with her. She didn't care, and I loved that about her so much.

"God, Joe," she whispered, twisting my fingers in hers. They were so cold, it was like she'd drowned in freezing water. "You're so warm, and I'm so cold." And Lissy smiled, so bloody beautiful that I wanted to cry, but she was already stepping away. Great waves of hot shame rolled over me. I'd always known it'd be like this, that she wouldn't feel the same, but I'd not expected it to actually hurt, to really feel like my internal organs were all being stirred with some kind of giant knife.

"I love you. I've always loved you." I'd no pride any more, so there was no saving that. I just came right out and said it, even though there was no point any more.

She didn't even try to pretend not to know what I was on about. "Joe," Lissy whispered. "I can't. I can't love you back."

"It's all right, you daft cow. I know. You're immortal." And God, it cost me a lot to say that. I laughed, which to be honest wasn't that hard because really I was laughing at myself. Losing my life over her for six whole years. Failing every exam I'd ever taken just because all I could see was her face. Giving up on everything, all because of her. And it was all for nothing. She didn't need me like I needed her. I felt cold. Completely cold, like I was already dead.

And then, suddenly, Connie spoke, butting in. "What the

hell is that?" she said, looking up at the sky. "What are they all staring at?" She was right, though: the Hidden surrounding us were no longer paying any attention to Lissy and me. They were all watching the sky, and through the numb misery I noticed for the first time what a state Connie was in, how she was having to hold her school shirt across her chest because all the buttons had been ripped off, and how her face was streaked with tears, and how she had that bloody awful hunted look in her eyes. Lissy must've got to her just in time – the Hidden were always hungry for mortals, wanting to touch us, to hold us, to feel the warmth. Deep, hot rage welled up inside me. She was just a kid, and one of them had blatantly attacked her.

"You shouldn't be here. You shouldn't be involved in this at all." It came out angry, not like I actually cared.

"Shut up," Connie hissed. "Look, Joe."

Lissy was no longer paying either one of us any attention. All the Hidden were watching the sky with complete concentration, and we were both forgotten like new toys bought for a spoilt kid.

Connie's eyes must've been sharper than mine, because it was a good few seconds before I could see anything up there at all. For a few moments, I had no idea what they were all staring at, and then a black speck appeared like a fleck of dust against the blue, bigger with every second until I could just make out the form of a bird hurtling towards the ground, claws jutting out ready to snatch some small creature from the ground. It swooped down into the clearing, hurtling towards Lissy so fast that Connie screamed and without even thinking what the hell I was doing I reached out and grabbed her, hauling her close to me. She clung on, her fingers digging into my arm.

"Get back!" I yelled, expecting the falcon to claw Lissy's face, so close that I could see the golden fury in its eyes. "Lissy, move!" I roared, furious at her for just standing there, watching, but at the second I was sure the falcon was about to attack her, suddenly it was just gone. There was only a boy standing in the clearing, face to face with her, hair as red as fire torn back from his head by a sudden wind, dark Hidden eyes black with rage. And his face was the mirror image of Lissy's, and I'd not seen him for more than six years. And she'd killed his father – *their* father. Larkspur.

"Oh, my God," Connie whispered, and she was shaking and so was I. "Oh, my God, Joe. What the hell is going on? *Who is he?*"

I didn't even know where to start so I kept my mouth shut. It wasn't exactly the moment to intervene – the long-lost sister and banished brother reunited just after she'd murdered their father. The assembled Hidden watched in complete silence, and I could sense a great tension mounting, like the air had thickened, and it was harder and harder to breathe.

"Larkspur," Lissy said, quietly. "You came home."

"There is no home." His voice shook with fury, and I saw that his face was wet with tears, which kind of surprised me after all the Swan King had done to him. "Not any more, Lissy. You killed him. Didn't you? You killed our father. I saw his death reflected in the sea; I watched him bleed into the waves."

"I had no choice." I hardly recognized Lissy's voice: she

136

sounded so cold, so inhuman. "Everyone lied to my sister and she had no idea what she was dealing with. Who she was dealing with. Connie opened the Gateway. It wasn't her fault."

"What are you talking about?" Connie demanded, her voice shaking just like Larkspur's. "I don't know what you mean – all I did was move a stupid iron cross from by the kitchen window. I kept having these dreams and I thought I was going mad, OK? Seeing this boy, all the time. All I wanted to do was prove to myself I wasn't going crazy, imagining things—"

"That boy was my father, mine and Lissy's," Larkspur spat. "And now he's dead. You should never have opened the Gateway. He was safe before: they all were, even if they were prisoners. Now you've let them out what do you think is going to happen?"

"I didn't let anyone out of anything!" Connie turned to look up at Lissy, and said, "*What?* Who is he, anyway?" When I saw the look on Connie's face I began to realize just how badly we'd screwed up by not telling her the truth about any of this. Her mouth just crumpled, like she'd been completely betrayed. All the time, the rest of the Hidden watched in silence, hundreds of them. Waiting to see what would happen next, and all the time Connie was still clinging to my arm like I was stopping her drowning, staring at Larkspur with utter hatred in her eyes.

Out of the silence a voice spoke: "Larkspur! Larkspur! Larkspur! The true heir has returned. The true heir has returned."

"Take the throne, then," Lissy hissed at him. "I don't want

137

it. I never wanted it. They tricked me – Iris and the others. They just used me as a way to escape."

"It was a fool's gambit," Larkspur snapped. "How long do you think it will be before the Fontevrault realize the Hidden are free? Now they're no longer prisoners, after all that's happened, the Fontevrault will have no excuse not to slaughter every last one of the Hidden."

"We'll send an envoy," Lissy replied. "We'll hold another covenant. Now that our father is dead, we can persuade the Fontevrault the Hidden mean no harm."

"For all that's worth! The last time we held a covenant with the Fontevrault they killed my mother." Larkspur's voice rang around the clearing as he swept all the assembled Hidden with one furious gaze. "Why did you make her do this? Do you not remember what happened the last time we tried to strike a bargain with the mortals? The Fontevrault cut my mother's throat in the woods outside Fontevrault Abbey and she died in agony."

Not one of the Hidden answered. And I for one knew that even if Larkspur dragged all the Hidden I could see back down into the Halls where they belonged, there were others who had already staked their claim to freedom. I'd passed at least six of them just getting here. A weird, jumpy sense of panic spread through me: the Hidden were out of control. They were just everywhere.

"He's her brother," Connie said, in this funny, quiet voice that shook just enough to betray how close she was to losing it completely. "That boy. That *thing*. He's Lissy's brother. Isn't he?"

No one replied.

"Larkspur," Lissy said. "I didn't want this any more than you do. Are you going to help me or not?"

"You're my queen as well as my sister, and I'm bound by loyalty – even though I don't choose it," Larkspur snapped. "No matter what you've done, how can I not help you?"

Connie tore away from my side and pelted off into the trees, leaving a peculiar silence behind her, because no one had really been taking much notice of her up till that point, not even Lissy, even though Connie was the one who'd started all this.

"Joe?" Lissy said, pleading, and I couldn't believe that after not seeing her little sister for years, Lissy wasn't even planning on going after her. It was going to be my job: the bloody dirty work, as usual.

"All right. You've got more important stuff to deal with." I didn't even bother keeping the bitterness out of my voice. I just ran, taking off through the trees and leaving Lissy and Larkspur to fight it out with the Hidden. At that moment, I wasn't even sure if I cared if the Fontevrault came thundering down to the Reach to destroy every last one of them. Lissy couldn't die, anyway, so what did it matter? Nothing bloody mattered.

Connie wasn't hard to follow, crashing and sobbing through the trees. She was fast, though, I'd grant her that, and by the time I caught up with her I was sweating and knackered. She'd curled herself up in a ball at the foot of a chestnut tree, arms wrapped tight around her knees, head down.

I sat down beside her, suddenly relieved just to stop, just

to rest. "Con?" I didn't even know where to start. She'd been lied to and lied to by her own family till it must've seemed like she couldn't trust anyone or anything. All I could think of was how many years I'd wasted, obsessing over Lissy. Nothing had seemed to matter except her, not school, not exams, not even my mates, who, if I'm honest, had all drifted away, leaving me in my own little world of dreaming and dreaming about Lissy, Lissy, Lissy. Always bloody Lissy. All for nothing. She didn't give a toss. How was it possible for me to want her so much, so bloody much, if I was nothing but a mate to her, or not even that, just a stepbrother she'd hardly known? How was it possible for me to have made such an idiot out of myself for so long? The Hidden and mortals are a bad combination. A really, really bad combination.

For what seemed like ages, Connie didn't speak at all. "She's not dead." Her voice was muffled, forehead still resting on her knees. "You know what?" Connie went on, still using that odd little shaky voice that sounded nothing like her normal cocky self. "I never believed she was dead. I really didn't. All those years I thought I was going crazy." She let out a short, sharp laugh. "All those sessions with that stupid counsellor. I can't believe they did that to me, Mum and Dad. Letting me think I was going mad just because they didn't want to tell me the truth."

"They were wrong. They were downright stupid. They should've told you the truth, and then we wouldn't be in this mess. You'd not have opened the Gateway if you'd have known what it'd mean."

"He's her brother," Connie said, still not looking up.

140

"That thing is her brother. He *flew*." She let out a funny little laugh. "I can't get over that Lissy's got a brother I never knew about. I mean, I guessed years ago that Dad wasn't her real dad, but a brother? I can't believe no one ever told me." She glanced up at me, and her face was stained with tears. "That's not even the weirdest thing about all this, though, is it? What *are* they, Joe? That Larkspur is the same as the boy I saw in my Dream – the one who told me to move the iron cross. His hair's different but they look so alike. I thought it was just a stupid dream, but I've done something really, really bad, haven't I?" She drew in a long, shuddering breath. "I've really messed up."

"It's not stupid, Con. You weren't to know. The boy you must've seen wasn't a boy at all – he's the Swan King, Larkspur's father – Lissy's father. He wanted to kill us all, to take revenge because his wife was murdered by mortals – it's why he got you to open the Gateway; they were trapped down there, in the Halls – but Lissy must have killed him, instead, before he got the chance to escape. They're the Hidden, and to be honest I still don't really know what they are. They don't age like us – they don't die normally, and iron's the only thing that can kill them – but the Hidden can't have children of their own. Larkspur was the last pure Hidden child to be born, and he's two thousand years old. They can't breed properly, not with each other, anyway. It's why they've always wanted us – mortals – and why we're not meant to have any contact with them. There was this group set up to keep us apart – like a security agency, but a really ancient one that's been around for hundreds of years: the

Fontevrault. They're the ones who killed the Swan King's wife. The Hidden are supposed to be trapped, imprisoned – the Swan King wanted to spread this plague to wipe us all out, to punish us in revenge. That's why your parents lied to you – they must've been afraid that you were too young to know the truth, that you couldn't be expected to keep it a secret, and the Fontevrault would go after you. Oh, Christ, Connie. It's a long story. Look, we should get back to the house. It's not safe out here. Not with the Hidden everywhere."

Lissy had killed the Swan King.

Connie looked up at me. I'd expected her to still be in tears, but her eyes were now dry and furious. "I'm not going anywhere, Joe."

"I'm not even sure I should be telling you this – your mam and dad obviously never wanted you to know."

"Joe, I've just discovered that my dead sister isn't really dead. Or human. There's not much point in you trying to whitewash this now. I think it's time someone told me the truth, don't you?"

I could've killed Miriam and Adam; if they'd only told Connie the real story years ago instead of spinning all those pathetic lies about Lissy being dead, we would never have been in this mess. She'd have known not to open the Gateway.

I sighed. "It's not good, all right. Now the Hidden have escaped, the Fontevrault will be coming. It's not going to take them long to pick up on this. They're all about not letting anyone know about the Hidden, to stop us mixing with them. I mean, you can see why – imagine if Hitler and the Nazis had managed to breed a load of hybrid Hidden immortal children just like Lissy. And to be fair, the last anyone knew including the Fontevrault was that Lissy and Larkspur's father wanted all the mortals dead. Every last one of us – in revenge for killing Larkspur's mother. It was hundreds of years ago, but time doesn't mean anything to the Hidden. They never forget. And once the Fontevrault hear the Gateway's open – and it won't be long before they find out – they'll come down here ready for a fight with the Swan King. They'll kill all the Hidden just to make sure they don't cause any trouble."

"Then why don't we just *let* these Fontevrault people kill them?" Connie demanded, her voice harsh. "They don't exactly seem like the most desirable neighbours, Joe."

"Because if all the Hidden were killed that would be genocide, Connie. Murder on a huge scale. And we'd be just letting it happen, that's why."

Connie stared at me for a second. "Then get someone to stop these Fontevrault people coming if you want to protect those Hidden things, though God knows why you do. It's our land, it's the Reach. The Fontevrault can't just turn up. They're not the police."

"They're bigger than the police – the whole operation is ratified by the government, even though no one official would ever admit to knowing about them."

Connie laughed. "Do you realize how ridiculous this sounds? It's like one of those conspiracy theories about the whole planet being an alien spaceship."

I gave her a sarcastic smile. "Yes, Connie, and what you've

just seen in the woods was bloody Tinkerbell and all her friends playing with Bambi."

"How do you even know about all this stuff, anyway, Joe?"

I let out a long breath. I wasn't sure where to start with that. "It's a long story. But your dad's one of them, Connie. Adam's one of the Fontevrault, and he kept Lissy a secret from them for fourteen years. I reckon you'll be seeing him sooner than you thought."

"Dad?" hissed Connie, and I realized I'd gone too far, that it was all just too much. "My dad's a member of this group?" she went on, furious. "More lies and more stupid secrets, more and more? Is there anything at all about my life that's actually true? Is there anything about my family that's in any way *normal*?"

Something inside her seemed to snap and she got up and ran, stumbling away through the trees in her school uniform. "Connie!" I shouted. "Come on, don't do this – I thought you wanted to know the truth. Just let me explain."

But she was gone, and I'd messed up again. Poor kid. Poor bloody kid. I got to my feet and ran after her, but I knew even then that Connie wasn't about to make it easy for me to find her. How could I even blame her?

19

Lissy

Night creeps closer and Larkspur and I stand alone on the lawn, watching the sun bleed red light into the sky behind the Reach. Fury and grief still seep from him like liquor from rotten meat. I'm about to go home, home at last, but in the back of my mind, all I can hear is our father saying, *Lissy, please*, over and over again. He was so desperate to die, for it all to be over. So why do I feel so numb? I killed him. I'm a murderer, taken in by another Hidden trick. By *Iris* – the only one I trusted. The only one apart from Larkspur who'd tried to help poor Tippy all those hundreds of years ago. And I'd felt so sorry for her.

"I don't want to go in," Larkspur says, quietly. "I've never trusted the mortals."

I shiver beneath my cloak of feathers, a warm soft weight hanging from my shoulders. It's part of me, feather shafts protruding from my shoulders, growing out of my flesh as if they've always been there. "I'm just as scared as you are. The Hidden are everywhere, Larkspur. I haven't seen Iris since we came through the Gateway – I don't know what she's planning – and so many others are unaccounted for. We should have sent everyone back to the Halls and sealed the Gateway. I need to make sure Connie's OK, then somehow get a message to the Fontevrault, or to my – to Adam Harker."

I'd nearly said, *my dad*. But Adam Harker has never been my true father. He's Fontevrault, though, and if anyone can help us now it's him. We need to negotiate.

Larkspur just gives me a long look I can't read the meaning of.

"I didn't want this, you know," I snap. "I didn't ask to be Queen. They got Iris to trick me. You know as well as I do she's got her own reasons for wanting to get out of the Halls, that she was the only one I'd trust, because of Tippy."

"Then let us hope that the mothers of Hopesay Edge close every window tonight, Lissy." Larkspur's voice is like glass. "Let us hope that they bolt every door."

"Are you coming or not?" I stalk towards the house, guilt giving way to anger. How could he possibly think I *wanted* this?

The front door opens before we even reach it. Joe stands there waiting, light pouring out from behind him, and another wave of pure guilt rolls over me. How much of his life has he wasted pining over me? I'm poison. I destroy everything I touch.

I swallow, hard. "Where's my mum?" At last, at last.

Joe shakes his head. "They're away."

Cold disappointment rolls over me, crushing. I've waited so long to see Mum – so *long* – and now she's not even here.

"Where's Connie? I need to see her." I can't forget my terror the first time I touched the world of the Hidden, years ago, that early-summer night at a lonely countryside railway station, getting off at the wrong stop and finding Larkspur waiting for me. How confused Connie must be, and how frightened.

"In her room. She won't speak to anyone, and I don't blame her." Joe steps back to let us past, and Larkspur visibly shudders as he stands in the hallway. There must be iron somewhere in the fabric of the front door – old nails, perhaps. It's not the first time he's been inside the Reach. In the back of my mind I still remember waking to find him sitting at the foot of my bed all those years ago.

Joe shuts the door, pushing home the bolt as if that could possibly keep out the evil waiting beyond the Reach. "Listen." His voice is harsh with emotion: regret, sorrow, shame. "Lissy, your dad's already here – Adam."

And now I'm so cold with horror that I'm glad Larkspur speaks for me on this one occasion: "So, do the Fontevrault know the Hidden are free?"

Joe shrugs. "How should I know? Adam's just as much of a liar as the rest of them. He's not said anything about the Hidden or the Fontevrault, and he's here alone. Said he came to see Connie. About an exam she was meant to take at school, and didn't. That's all."

Relief floods through me, but Joe's right. Adam could have been lying. Perhaps the Fontevrault already know the Hidden are loose and are waiting, hidden, ready to destroy them all?

"They'll kill us." Larkspur speaks with quiet finality. "Even if the Fontevrault find out my father is dead, they'll still kill all the Hidden rather than risk the rest of the mortals discovering us."

We need to see Adam now. He's our best chance of persuading the rest of the Fontevrault that the Hidden aren't a threat now the Swan King is dead. Connie will have to wait. "Where is he?" I whisper.

And Joe doesn't answer; he just leads us into the sitting room, and the battered red sofas and the ancient oak panelling on the walls are exactly the same, still studded with carved wooden roses. *Mum*. I've waited so long to see her, and now she's not even here. Joe crosses over to the far wall, pushing one of the wooden roses. With a gentle creak, a section of the panelling swings inwards, letting in a shaft of weak electric light that Larkspur recoils from. It's so strange seeing him indoors, as if a wild red deer had just wandered into someone's dining room. I want to comfort him somehow, he looks so wretched, but how can I when I'm the cause of his misery? Larkspur will never sit at his father's side again, all because of me.

The familiar battered furniture hasn't changed at all – it's as if I've been gone five minutes, not six years, as if I might walk into the kitchen and find an eight-year-old Connie making chocolate Pop-Tarts, burning crumbs of sugary icing in the toaster. But the real Connie is in her bedroom. I imagine her trying to absorb the knowledge that her own parents have been lying to her for years, that they allowed her to think she was going mad rather than admit I was still alive, but a prisoner of the Hidden. And now I'm a murderer, too. Connie would be better off without having me for a sister.

"Do you live here now, Joe?" My voice sounds small and stupid, like I'm just a precocious ten-year-old making conversation at a cocktail party.

Joe jerks his head. "No." As if it was the most idiotic question ever. "I never come here if I can help it."

In hostile silence we follow him into what must be an old servants' corridor, Larkspur leading the way, black cloak surging around his ankles. It's a warren of dilapidated rooms out here with dusty windows and unlit passages home to stacks of broken chairs, piles of forgotten books and letters. No one ever comes here now, it's clear – not until today – and I can't help wondering how on earth Joe has managed to discover all this if he hardly ever comes to the Reach. He must have been shown the way by someone who knows this place far better than either of us, and I remember how Mum lived here alone with Miles when their parents were dead, and how Adam was Miles's best friend, here almost every day, all those parties. It must have been a wild time – three teenagers with the run of an ancient manor house – a time of magic that turned into a nightmare when Miles opened the Gateway. We must be in the oldest part of the house now – the ceilings are so low that Larkspur and I can't stand at our full height, and the few windows we pass are nothing but slits in thick walls built of old, old stone.

Joe stops before a battered door, white paint peeling off like wet scabs. "In here." His voice is hard and clipped: he holds the door open without even looking at me.

Larkspur moves to walk in but I lay a hand on his arm,

trying to ignore the way he flinches as if even my touch disgusts him.

Don't. I speak right into his mind. *The Fontevrault might have come with iron – you said yourself we can't trust them, not even Adam Harker. Let me go first.*

He doesn't reply and I've no idea if Larkspur has closed his mind off to me completely, but either way he stands back to let me past.

"Lissy, be careful," Joe says, quietly.

I turn and smile at him. "Idiot. What can he do to me?"

I'm ready to meet the Fontevrault: I'm ready to meet the man I always thought was my father. I walk into a long, low-ceilinged chamber with a row of tiny windows along one wall – again, they're more like arrow-slits in a castle. There's a table laid out in the middle of the room, and here he is.

"*Lissy.*" Adam speaks my name but doesn't move from his seat behind the scrubbed wooden table. He looks older, his hair thinner on top than I remember and completely grey now. It's a shock. "Lissy," he says again, as if testing out the shape of the letters in his mouth. He stares at me from head to toe with a kind of bemused horror. *It's probably the cloak*, I think. *A feather overkill.* Which makes me want to laugh as if I am a girl again, not a queen.

I can't help staring right back at him, tracing over every line of his face, every detail: the tanned skin, the slant of his nose and the faint chicken-pox scar on his left ear he'd once told me was a fairy's kiss. I hardly know what to say. I'm numb, frozen. Wasn't there a time, long ago, when me and Dad didn't speak, and didn't that cut me to the quick? Some silly and unimportant thing – I discovered he was having an affair, that's it. I found a letter, a card. I can still remember the look in his eyes when I said, *Who's she?* Pure irritation. I think that was the first moment I knew I wasn't really his child: that I couldn't be. He would never have looked at me like that if I were. He never would have looked at Rafe and Connie with such an expression in his eyes. I knew. I sense Joe and Larkspur at my back, waiting, and I step forwards.

"Lissy?" Dad says again, and it feels wrong to think of him in that way now – he's not *Dad* any more. He's just Adam Harker. My real father is dead. I killed the Swan King: I cut his face and I poisoned him with iron. Adam gets to his feet, stumbling a little against the carved wooden chair, and there's a silence in which we're meant to hug. But we don't; we just stand there staring at each other. It's been too long, and things have changed too much. He's one of the Fontevrault, and I'm here to negotiate with him – that's all.

"Is it only you?" I ask, and the words hang in the air between us.

Adam nods. "For now, Lissy."

Larkspur glances from Adam to me and back again, his eyes dark with grief. "You hid her from the rest of the Fontevrault for fourteen years," he says. "You betrayed them. Why do the Fontevrault trust you alone with Lissy, Adam Harker?"

Adam watches him carefully across the table, studying Larkspur with some fascination, his eyes travelling from my brother to me and back again, tracing the way our features echo each other's. "They don't trust me, but they don't know

I'm here, either. Given that we're all still alive and there's no immortal plague, I assume that your father is either dead or has changed his mind about taking his revenge on the mortal race?" I can't tell if he's being serious or mocking the Swan King, and I'm surprised to find how angry it makes me.

"I killed him." My voice rings out in the silence.

Adam flinches, a muscle in his jaw tightening as if I've just committed a terrible faux pas at a dinner party. So there's still some part of this man that sees me as his daughter: murder is not a suitable pastime for a well-brought-up girl in the Harker family, even if the victim in question was his worst and most hated enemy.

"The Hidden only want their freedom, nothing else," I go on. "The Hidden have been in darkness for too long. They need light. Now that the Swan King is dead, there's no reason the Hidden can't be free. We don't wish any harm on the mortals."

Except perhaps Iris, with her all-consuming desire for a child. Except perhaps Briar, with his unhealthy desire to hold a mortal girl—

Larkspur says nothing, but I can't help uneasily wondering where Iris is. I try to ignore a vivid memory of Briar with his hands on Connie, desperate for the warmth of her body. It hadn't been easy to make Briar leave her alone. I'd had to use all the force I could muster, all the skills my father taught me. Will I really be able to control the Hidden roaming free in the world with so many mortal temptations close at hand?

"If the Swan King really is dead, that does change things – or at least I hope it does," Adam says.

"If you're one of the Fontevrault, can't you do anything to stop them coming after my people?"

My people. The Hidden. Despite everything, despite how the Hidden used me, how I loathe them in so many ways, I've become one of them, and the cold shock of it jolts through me. They need me. They depend on me.

Adam looks at me across the table, and it feels like he and I are the only ones in the room. He was my dad once, but I'm trading on old loyalties now. "I'll ask your brother to raise a false alarm," Adam says, and I stare at him, confused. How will Larkspur be able to help? He's pure Hidden: he holds even less currency with the Fontevrault than I do.

Adam shakes his head, looking at me with something approaching pity. "*Rafe*," he says. "Your brother Rafe, Lissy. He lives in India now – if he alerts the rest of the Fontevrault to a Hidden sighting out there, it'll be enough to divert their attention for a short while – they'll be horrified at just the suspicion that even one of you has managed to escape the Halls."

Rafe. I'd genuinely forgotten him: my own mortal brother.

"Keep the Hidden away from mortal places as much as you can – if news of any other sightings filters back to the rest of the Fontevrault, I won't be able to help you. Larkspur is right – they don't trust me." Adam lifts his gaze, fixing his eyes on my face. "The Fontevrault might not be able to kill you, Lissy, but they certainly don't want anyone else to know that you were ever born, that you were even possible. They'll keep you prisoner, so whatever happens, make sure you're not caught."

It's just what the Swan King said to me: *It's not my wish for you to be kept prisoner till the end of time.* And I push away the mental image of being held in some kind of laboratory until one by one the last humans on earth die and the walls crumble around me. I shiver, wrapping the hawk-feathers closer around my shoulders.

"All right, then. We'll stay hidden."

"You should return to the Halls," Adam says, sharply. "You'll be safe there if you allow us to seal the Gateway after you. *If* you ensure it's not opened again, Lissy."

"*No.*" Larkspur and I both answer at the same instant. I never want to set foot in the Halls of the Hidden again. It's nothing but a place of darkness, of sorrow, tunnels littered with rotten finery and the bones of mortals who never found the way out. I never want to walk those tunnels again. I never want to taste the soily tang of that stale, dark air. Never.

"We'll hide," I go on, speaking so fast and so firmly that Adam doesn't have the chance to interrupt. "There aren't many wild places in the world, but there are enough for us."

"Then you'll have to *stay* hidden," Joe says, brusque as ever. "The Fontevrault aren't going to stop hunting you down just because the Swan King's dead: if you believe that, you've even less sense than I thought."

"They won't find us. No mortal will ever find us." Larkspur replies before I open my mouth. "We must leave now and gather the tribe, ready to flee."

"No," Adam says, again. "You can't hide. You'll have to return to the Halls, Lissy."

I stare at Adam a moment. I'm so much taller now. "Never.

It's never going to happen. The Hidden will not return to the Halls, and that is my final word on the matter. Where do you propose we gather?" I look my brother in the eye, daring him to meet my gaze. Sooner or later, he'll have to, no matter how much he despises me. "In the woods again?"

Larkspur shakes his head, still refusing to look at me. "No. Joe is right. We're supposed to be in hiding – we want the Fontevrault to know that we can live in the mortal world without disturbing anyone, without even being seen, just as we did for fourteen years before the Swan King claimed you, Lissy. The forest isn't safe. There is sacred ground in Hopesay Edge beyond the boundaries of the Reach. It's not bound by the power of the old standing stones like the house is, but by the trees themselves."

I want to argue that there are plenty of trees in the woods, but I wait in what I hope is dignified silence for him to continue.

"The yew trees," Larkspur goes on, impatient because I don't understand, because most of our father's great knowledge died with him at the moment I took his life. "In the churchyard – it's been sacred ground since long before the church was raised from wood and then stone. The trees are more than two thousand years old and they hold their own power – they can't protect us from the edge of an iron weapon, but lych-yard yews have always offered their own measure of concealment for the Hidden. Any mortal who chances past won't easily see us gathered there. We'll appear as nothing more than a trick of the light, just shifting shadows."

"You'll be safer in the Halls," Adam insists. "On the side

of the Gateway where you belong, Lissy. You'll be truly protected there – the Fontevrault wouldn't follow if they knew you were safely concealed down there, even if they were able to find their way through the tunnels."

"Listen. The Hidden will *never* return to the Halls – give them their freedom and they'll leave you all alone. That's all we want." I stare at him, willing him to agree with me. He's got to. He's our only chance. "Consider this, Adam – how could we ever be sure that the Fontevrault wouldn't decide to invade the Halls and attack us? The Gateway only binds the Hidden – any mortal could cross over. It was probably only their fear of my father's plague that stopped the Fontevrault invading and killing the Hidden before now."

Adam watches me a moment, then at last he nods. "If that's what you want, Lissy. But if you're seen, if the Hidden are spotted in the outside world, I won't be able to help you."

"That's fair. The churchyard, then. I'll gather the Hidden there, and we'll leave Hopesay by dawn." I turn back to Larkspur, daring him to look away this time, meeting the full force of the fury and hatred in his eyes. "Will you help me bring them? We'll be able to act more quickly together."

Larkspur nods, curt and cold. "I will do whatever it takes to protect the Hidden from mortal harm." He's never going to forgive me, and how can I blame him?

I turn back to Adam and Joe. "I'd like to see Connie before I go."

Adam frowns. He looks tired just at the mention of her name. "Absolutely not. I've already lost one daughter to the Hidden."

"I need to see her." Does he even know that Connie is Tainted, that she has abilities she does not understand? I could so easily hurl Adam from one end of this stone-cold room to the other without touching a hair of his head, and the anger is rising in me.

"He's Fontevrault," Larkspur cuts in, as if he has just seen the colour of my thoughts, his voice still so hard and cold. "Don't anger him. They can't be trusted as it is."

Joe glanced from Adam to me and back again. "Larkspur's right." He shot me a look, telling me to leave it.

Part of me wants to walk out of here right this minute and find Connie's room, to just take her with me. It's not as if any of them could stop me: after all the Swan King taught me, I doubt that even Larkspur could stand in my way if he chose to. But Larkspur is right: Adam Harker might have been my dad once, but he's still a member of the Fontevrault, and I'm here to negotiate our freedom. I'll find a way of reaching Connie. She needs my help; I've abandoned her once before and I won't do it again.

Adam stands up again, stepping awkwardly around the table, and I remember a day long ago when he took the stabilizers off my first bike, and he pushed me around the garden with one of his hands warm against my back, and finally he said, *Go on, then, Tinkerbell – it's your turn now.* I remember pedalling so hard, so fast that I just kept going and when I finally crashed into the lilac tree at the bottom of the garden, all I could hear was him whooping and shouting, *Go Lissy,* as if I'd just won a marathon, not fallen off my bike. And yet even in this dark room, in a lonely and forgotten corner of Hopesay Reach, I feel like I can smell white lilac flowers, and see the petals tumbling slowly to the grass, tangling in my hair. But that was then, and this is now. He was my dad, but not any more.

Larkspur speaks to me without opening his mouth for the first time since I killed the Swan King. *You've secured our freedom for now, if we can trust him. Time is running out.* He might hate me, he might wish that I could die so that he could kill me, but he is right: we've got to go. Connie will have to wait. It's time to rein in the Hidden, to herd them to the safety of the yew trees in Hopesay churchyard before we run for ever.

20

Connie

I paced over to my bedroom window and sat on the sill, wet hair dripping down my back, tucking my legs up beneath me as I looked out over the green blanket of woodland, all spread with a layer of thick grey mist. I shivered. It was like I could still feel the Hidden boy's hands on me, his cold, cold hands, and no matter how long I stayed under the jets of hot water I'd never be clean again. I shivered uncontrollably. If Lissy hadn't been there, if she hadn't come, what would he have done, that boy? The sky was clearing a little now, strands of cloud touched by the setting sun. The party was meant to be starting. They'd all be arriving soon – maybe there were already cars in the lane, kids cadging lifts off older brothers and sisters, some of them cycling down the lanes, some even walking. A party was a party – people would do pretty much anything to make sure they got there.

My phone bleeped and I glanced down at a text from Blue. *Are you crazy? We can't stop it now.* I'd known all along that there was nothing I could do, that they'd all just come, but I had to try something, and I'd been texting Blue all day saying we should call the whole thing off, but I couldn't give him a believable reason why not. The woods were full of creatures. Not-human things. Lissy-things. How was I supposed to explain that?

She's not human. She's not dead but she's not human either.

I couldn't just let all my friends and half my school and probably most of the teenagers in the county walk into the woods expecting a party and find those creatures waiting for them. In the back of my mind I could still see the boy who touched me – the curve of his lips, those weird dark grey eyes glittering like cold metal.

I heard the stairs creak: footsteps. Someone was coming. My mouth was so dry. I honestly felt like my blood had been replaced with frozen water. My heart raced as I stepped across my bedroom floor, tugging clothes almost at random from the heap by my bed, pulling on a long glittery skirt over my leggings, the one I'd worn on Christmas Eve, that time when I'd drunkenly tried to seduce Joe. I cringed at the memory of his horrified face, grabbing a stripey T-shirt and red sweatshirt. Just as I reached for the door handle, someone knocked, and I couldn't stop myself jumping. Taking one long breath as I pulled the sweater on over my T-shirt, I said, "*What?*"

There was nothing Joe could say to me now. He'd lied to me just as everyone else had done. He'd had his chances to tell the truth about Lissy and he'd never taken them. But when the door creaked open, it wasn't Joe standing in the hallway, it was my dad, and he didn't look happy. Cold horror trickled through me.

Dad.

"Elena let you out, then?" I snapped, suddenly flooded with white-hot rage, not caring why or how he was even at the Reach. They'd all lied to me. Everyone in my family. My mother, my father. Rafe. Joe. Every single one of them.

"Connie, don't," Dad said, quietly.

"Oh, shut up!" I roared, unable to control my rage. "What do you want, anyway? Why are you even here?"

Mrs Anderson must have phoned him after all. Traitor. I wondered if he realized how much I knew.

Dad stepped into the room, forcing me to step backwards and away from him. But instead of turning round and tearing strips off me for not taking the exam, he just sat on my unmade bed as if he'd run out of strength to stand. "Con, we really, really need to talk—"

He knew that I knew. I'd found them all out, unwrapped all those carefully placed lies.

"You could have fooled me!" My voice filled the room again, loud and ragged with rage, so huge that it scared me. Suddenly I couldn't stop crying, tears spilling uncontrollably down my face. And just at that moment, Dad looked up, as if he'd only just seen me properly for the first time.

"You don't understand, Connie – just let me explain—" I couldn't face this now. More lies, probably. His excuses would just have to wait.

"I don't want to hear it. Just leave me alone."

"No. We really need to talk about this, Con. About Lissy. About what happened. You must have a lot of questions – you must be really confused— *Please.*"

And so he'd decided that finally I was allowed to hear

161

the truth about my own sister. After all the lies they'd told me. After letting me think I was going crazy for refusing to believe that she was dead.

For a second I was burning, then freezing. The words just boiled out of me. "You don't get to choose!" I screamed. "You don't get to control when I just sit down and listen. You all lied to me, *you made me think I was going crazy*, now go away. I don't want to hear any more of your bullshit. You're a liar and a cheat, and I never want to see you again."

"I'm sorry, Connie. We did what we thought was best. All we wanted was to protect you." Dad just turned around and walked silently out of my room, closing the door behind him, leaving me feeling deflated and even weirder than before. I listened to the creaking floorboards as he walked along the landing, down the stairs, and the silence once he'd gone seemed bigger than ever before, filling the entire Reach as if it was separate from the rest of the world, lost in its own silent universe.

I hauled myself back up onto my windowsill seat, wrapping both arms around my knees because my hands were shaking so much, and late-evening light slanted in through the leaded window, leaving a bright puddle on an Indian rug that had belonged to my great-grandmother. My eyes were dry and hot with anger, but I refused to let myself cry. I was already late to my own party.

How the hell was I going to get up to the woods without Dad or Joe noticing? I glanced out of the window. I'd got out that way before, hanging on to the ivy and praying that it wouldn't tear off the side of the house. I was already dressed and ready to go, except for the fact the only footwear in my bedroom was a pair of fluffy slipper socks I'd had since I was twelve. Not ideal for a stand-off in the woods.

Pretty much my entire school was heading up to the Reach, and only I knew what was out there waiting for them. *Who* was out there... What were they, really, those people? All so tall and beautiful. Almost human, but not. I did the only thing I could do, under the circumstances: I texted Blue and then Amy, begging for wellies, and I climbed out of my bedroom window.

I had to go. There was no choice.

PART TWO

THE HIDDEN RUN FREE

21

Lissy

I stretch my hawk-wings in the summer evening sky, rising above woodland that spreads like a swathe of rumpled green cloth right beyond Hopesay Reach. The Hidden are roaming free amongst the trees, and God knows how much further beyond them. Have they strayed into the village? Have they been spotted? I must get them to the churchyard – to the shelter of the ancient yew trees. I wish flight wasn't the royal gift of the Hidden, that we could all take bird-form, but even as the thought crosses my mind, a childhood memory drifts through my head: Dad and Rafe traipsing off over the fields every January, guns on their shoulders, relentless dull explosions ripping apart the clear winter skies, and dead pheasants lying on the kitchen table, their bright feathers drooping sadly. Even in bird-form, the Hidden would not be safe from the Fontevrault for long.

I can't stop thinking of Iris, imagining her drifting from cottage to cottage, silent as a shadow, listening outside each curtained window for the rapid, brand-new heartbeat of a human baby. Larkspur is on the wing, searching too. I can't get Adam's words out of my head: *If the Hidden are seen,*

I can't help you, Lissy. For now, thanks to him, it isn't even the Fontevrault I need to fear, not immediately, but the Hidden crossing paths with the mortals of Hopesay Edge once more. It never ends well.

It's only now that I realize the price of freedom will be to never stop running. We'll have to go far, maybe even across the sea, looking for those wild places where mortal people hardly ever go. There aren't many places like that left in the world. Untouched. Safe. And given how much force I spent tearing Briar away from Connie, I don't even know if the Hidden will listen to me … if they'll follow.

Larkspur's words roll around and around in my head like cold stones: *Then let us hope that the mothers of Hopesay Edge close every window tonight, Lissy. Let us hope that they bolt every door.*

I turn my hawk-gaze to the forest floor, and looking down, I realize with a breathless jump that one of the Hidden is right below me, stalking through the trees in complete silence. He's certainly Hidden – a dark-haired boy I don't immediately recognize – I would have noticed any human long before now, purely because of the noise. True quiet is a Hidden trait, and I've got to begin somewhere, even with just a single Hidden boy. I land in my girl-form, kicking up a swirl of dead leaves, the feathered cloak still an unfamiliar weight at my shoulders as it billows out around me, golden and brown, the cloak of a queen. I expect the Hidden boy to back away in shock, but he only stands and watches with that peculiar Hidden stillness, just a few metres away, his dark hair cut unusually short for one of the Hidden, hanging over his eyes as he looks me up and down from head to toe, taking in my royal cloak of hawk-feathers in total silence. His eyes are so dark I can't read their expression at all.

I've never seen him before.

He's not from the Halls. And as that realization dawns, so does another. He's not pale enough. His skin is golden-brown, almost suntanned, just like a mortal's. But everything else about him is Hidden – his height, his slender build, the graceful cheekbones. After six years trapped in the Halls, how can there be one Hidden face I don't recognize? There's something wrong. I don't like this.

"Who are you?" In answer, the boy only stares at me with undisguised contempt; I try again, unease rising up within me like nausea. *Who is he?* "Go to the churchyard and wait for me there – tell the same to any Hidden you meet on the way."

He smiles, but it's a vicious smile. "I only take orders from the Swan King." The smile disappears, and the golden-brown light seems to drain from his skin, leaving him whiter than old bone, and now he looks unmistakeably Hidden – there is no way he could ever be taken for a mortal now. *Who is he, who is he?* "But the Swan King is dead, isn't he, little girl? Dead and gone. Just feathers on the wind."

"It's what he wanted." The words fly out of my mouth so quickly. Why am I defending myself? "Who are you?" I repeat, keeping my voice steady now, ice-cold and regal.

Iris's words in the White Hall begin to make more sense. *Why not my baby?* I know now what she meant. I wasn't the only hybrid to have survived.

Why has no one ever told me?

And slowly, slowly, the half-breed boy steps towards me, totally unafraid. He knows what I am, who I am, because he's the same – a face on the other side of the same coin, another who can't die. Immortal like the Hidden, he will never be a victim to age or disease, but like me, he is also immune to the fatal touch of iron. And now I can feel it – red-hot hatred rolling across the clearing towards me, searing from his eyes, expressed in the cold rigidity of his shoulders, his stance. Hatred and utter, utter fury. It slams into me with the force of a blow, and I'm breathless, my cloak of golden feathers hanging at my shoulders, a weight I can't shake off.

"Who are you?" I demand again, my voice rising, and I can't disguise my panic.

"You don't need to know who I am, little girl." His voice shakes with rage – another mortal trait: there is too much raw emotion here for a pure-blooded Hidden. He's now standing so close that I can feel the warmth of his breath in my face, and I can see that although everything else about him is Hidden, this boy's eyes are still the bright brown of a new-ploughed field in autumn sunlight. Mortal eyes. The rest of the world seems to fall away, and all the woodland around me is silent.

"Why didn't they ever tell me there was another?" My voice is shaking. *I'm not the only one. Not the only hybrid.*

But the boy only gives me a hateful, bitter smile. "Maybe you just didn't need to know, little girl. If I were you I'd get your people away from here before the mortals kill them one by one. They do die very easily, you know, when struck with an iron weapon." He steps even closer, half a head taller than me. "Is being Queen harder than you thought, Lissy Harker?"

He knows my name.

I could lift one finger and hurl his body hard across this clearing just as I did to Briar. But I don't. There's another one like me. *A boy.* What was it the Swan King had said, the reason why he hadn't just taken my blood and brewed the plague when I was a prisoner of the Hidden as a baby, before Larkspur took me home? *Your blood needed to take on the richness of a grown woman's.* It's because I'm a girl, female. This boy, he's nothing but a failed experiment with the wrong cocktail of hormones in his blood. Whoever he is, why I was never told about him, it makes no difference now. He's just an outcast. A reject.

"No one told me because you don't matter," I whisper, but loud enough for him to hear – our faces are still just inches apart. "I don't know what you're doing here, but it's no concern of mine."

He's still smiling as I turn and walk away through the trees, hunting for the Hidden, for my people. I feel the heat of his gaze upon my back, burning through my cloak of feathers as he watches me go, and all I can do is pray he has no idea that had I not clenched my hands into fists, my fingers would be shaking.

22

Connie

The woods were quiet, tall trees pointing up at the sky like spears, bracken and nettles tangled below, catching around my legs as I walked; the soles of my feet raw with pain now after the barefoot walk up from the Reach. Early-summer evening light shafted down through gaps in the green canopy of leaves and branches, but I couldn't hear a single bird in the trees. At this time of year the woods around the Reach were normally echoing with birdsong, cuckoos calling and calling, such murdering careless birds, shoving blackbird eggs out of their nests and replacing them with their own. Young cuckoos are changelings just like Lissy – a not-human girl growing up in the heart of my own family, with a starring role in all my earliest memories. The day I started school, I went into the classroom with Lissy holding my hand.

I thought she was my sister.

My whole life was just an illusion, a carefully woven fabric of lies upon lies upon lies, and the woods were silent, and as I walked, not even caring any more about the twigs and stones digging into the soles of my bare feet, I couldn't stop the tears spilling down my face, as if crying could actually change anything or make it better.

It wasn't long before I heard laughter, though, a boy singing: Blue, ripping off a song that had been all over the radio the last couple of weeks. By the sound of it, he wasn't alone — I caught snatches of laughter, a girl joining in with the singing, a couple of voices I didn't recognize and someone swearing. Picking my way across a carpet of last year's dead leaves and pine cones, I found them all in the clearing where I'd met Lissy just a few hours earlier, where that beautiful, evil thing had put his hands on me. There was no sign of the Hidden now, as if all that had been nothing but a terrible dream.

Amy's boyfriend, Nye, had been true to his word and managed to get his white Transit van up one of the forestry tracks; everyone was unloading speakers while Amy sat on a blanket with Mika in his pram beside her, waving at me across the clearing. When I saw Mika in the pram rather than in Amy's arms, I fought the urge to run and bundle him into her lap where he'd be safe. The Hidden were everywhere, and maybe those old stories about babies were true. Lissy had been taken, after all, when she was just a baby.

Amy jumped up from the blanket she'd spread out on the dead leaves, leaving Mika still in his pram. "Connie! What the hell is going on?" She rushed over, staring down at my bare feet. "Er, would you like to elaborate?" She gave me a long look up and down, then hugged me. Hard. "Bloody hell, are you all right? You've been crying, haven't you? What's going on?"

"Mika," I said, trying to sound normal. "You should take him home, Ames. It's not safe up here."

She gave me a weird look. "Only last night you were trying to persuade me to bring him to the party. What's the matter?"

How on earth was I going to explain? She'd think I was crazy; she'd never believe me. "My dad turned up. He doesn't know I'm here – I had to sneak out without him knowing, and all my shoes were downstairs – that's why I asked you to bring boots." I pulled away, glancing across at Blue, who was sitting very close to Jessie. So close that their heads were almost touching. Neither of them seemed to have noticed me. I took a deep breath. "Listen, Amy, you've got to go. You and Mika—" I broke off. Everyone knew I'd been in counselling for nearly two years after Lissy died – no, after she *went* – and Amy was one of the few people in Hopesay who knew exactly why: that I hadn't accepted Lissy was dead. Amy also had no reason to believe that I wasn't a little delusional and damaged. I knew I'd have to tread carefully or she'd just write off everything I said. I took another long, shuddery breath. "Look, Amy – I just don't think it's going to be safe up here tonight, that's all."

"I'm not staying for the party, Con, you know that. What's the matter? Blue said you'd been texting him all afternoon wanting to call the whole thing off. Why?"

"There's some people coming that we didn't invite—"

Amy gave me a sarcastic smile. "You're not kidding. It was bound to happen, wasn't it? What did you expect, though, seriously? You're just going to have to go with it, Con. I'm sure they'll all just be up for a good time, whoever they are."

"No, really, listen. Blue doesn't know. Someone – someone

174

at school told me there's a load of really hardcore people coming. I'm properly scared, Amy. It's going to get genuinely out of control. I really think you and Mika should go home now."

Amy shrugged. "Well, that's my plan, anyway. Don't worry, Con – Nye's here and he's not going to let anything happen to me and Mika. I'll even get him to walk us home if that makes you happy. Listen, keep an eye on Blue, won't you?" She glanced over to where her brother was sitting, now arm in arm with Jessie. Amy smiled. "You do realize he's only glued to Jessie Mayhew because he's given up on you, right?" Amy reached out, squeezing my shoulder, and for a second I had to fight the urge to cry, just because I wished life was as simple as Amy thought, that I was only really upset because Blue was all over another girl.

"He's not my boyfriend," I said, quietly. "He's my best friend."

"That's always difficult with a guy and a girl, though, isn't it?" Amy reached over to Mika's pram and delved into the basket underneath, pulling out a pair of fleece socks and her green wellies covered with spray-painted silver dots – the ones she'd worn to Glastonbury the year before, when Mika was unheard of, and I'd got into the most spectacular amount of trouble for going with her because I was only thirteen. We'd caught the train, and throughout the whole journey I remember thinking how easy it would be to get off at the next stop and just go home, but I never did.

This time there wasn't even a train I could catch; there was no way of turning back.

23

Larkspur

I spread my falcon-wings, banking on currents of warm air. I sense Lissy's presence nearby, her rage, her panic, and looking down at the forest floor, I see a good number of the Hidden swarming westwards through the thinning trees, heading for the shelter of the lych-yard yews. Finally, here's Lissy herself at the back of the group, cloak of feathers tugging out behind as she lends an arm to an Elder: one of the White Hall guards I feared so much as a child, but who now needs to lean on her queen in order to keep up, blinded by sunlight, dizzied by fresh air, her black robes tangling and twisting in the dead leaves and broken branches.

Lissy, where are the rest? Briar, Iris — the others? I've hardly used her name since she killed our father, and it feels wrong, as if I've forgiven her, as if I no longer wish there was a way she too could die. She does not reply — her mind is silent, closed off from mine behind a white wall of cold fury. There's a handful of Hidden that I can't spot here — Briar for one, Iris for another, both totally unaccounted for — and as I land, taking on my Hidden-form again, I feel a clutch of fear within me that makes me wish I was still in my falcon-form.

The falcon is never afraid.

The trees are thinning now, the woodland giving way to a steep, grassy hillside tumbling down towards the lonely lights of Hopesay Edge, just a jumble of cottages huddling beneath an enormous night sky now lit by a rising full moon.

"Where are the rest? Briar? Iris?" I demand again, landing at Lissy's side as she helps the Elders negotiate the dew-damp grass, but she doesn't stop. She just carries on walking, turning at last to throw me a hateful glance over her shoulder.

What right has *she* got to be furious with me?

"Briar did not come when I called – not all the Hidden are loyal to me, Larkspur, in case you hadn't noticed." She sounds just like our father, her voice blank with rage.

"Did you really think Briar would answer your call after you humiliated him like that?" She'd hurled him across the clearing for putting his hands on her sister, just as my father once slammed her across the White Hall itself: not a punishment easily forgotten or forgiven, however much deserved.

"Why else do you think I asked for your help?" Lissy walks away, shepherding our people towards the churchyard without looking back at me. I am the one who is supposed to be furious with her, not the other way around.

I wish he were here, our father.

"I'll keep on searching." I know I should just turn and run with all my strength and speed towards the heart of the ancient woodland, that I can't fail this time, that I must find Iris before she does something stupid and gets hurt – and Briar too, for what he is worth – but the words leave my mouth before I have the chance to swallow them back. "What right do you have to be angry with me?"

Lissy stops again, and the Elder leaning on her arm slumps. We're running out of time. The weaker Hidden have no strength to fight angry mortals, and sooner or later, those mortals will come in panicked hordes, searching for their children. "Why did no one tell me?" Lissy turns to look at me over her golden-feathered shoulder, speaking in a furious hiss. "Why did no one ever say there was another one like me?"

Nicolas. Sheer, freezing-cold panic washes through me. He is here, and he has not told me, which means he is hiding something. An intention he knows I will try to stop him realizing. There is nothing in the world Nicolas can do to Lissy but make her suffer, and the only mortal on earth who Lissy loves with her whole heart, who never betrayed her even once is her sister. Connie. Connie, whose face Nicolas has seen in the water for weeks on end. He knows who she is, and I would give anything for my father to be here now because the Swan King was the only one Nicolas ever really listened to, his loyalty utterly wedded to my father. The Swan King is the only one on earth who could stop Nicolas now, and now he is gone, I am left to try.

Lissy is already walking away.

"Wait!" But Lissy doesn't wait for an answer; she just helps my father's old guard down the hillside towards the safety of the yew trees in the lych-yard.

And the truth is, if Nicolas finds Connie Harker before I do, he'll kill her.

24

Connie

The clearing was heaving – groups of people sitting around on the floor, even a few sitting up in the dark trees, smoking and laughing and kicking their legs. It was a clear night and I could see bright points of starlight between the mesh of branches. Music pounded on and on, beating in time with my heart and my blood. Blue was still glued to Jessie, and although I was always at the centre of a crowd of people, I was always alone.

"Why d'you keep wanting to stop all the fun, Connie?" Kyle Ayrshire shouted in my ear, flecking the side of my face with spit. "It's like, the party of the year, and after this we're all just going to be doing exams and getting old." He turned to the blurred faces around us – Blue and Jessie, Tia, everyone I hung out with at school. "You're a total hero, Connie Harker! Stop telling us to go home, OK?"

Jessie rolled her eyes. "She's spinning out, more like. Get a grip, Connie – no one's listening and every time you tell us all we should go home, everyone just thinks you're being a complete freak. Was it that bump on the head you got in maths? What was even going on with that, anyway?"

I stared at Jessie helplessly, trying to imagine what she would say if I told them the truth: *Oh, yeah. The whole maths thing… I'd just seen a vision of an immortal king who tricked me into letting him escape so that he could destroy the entire human race. Luckily my dead sister was around, who is neither dead nor human, and she murdered him before he got the chance.*

Blue frowned. I could tell he was totally confused. "She's not a freak, Jess, but you should just relax, Con."

All I could say – again – was, "Guys, we should get out of here. We should all go home." But none of them could hear me, the music and the shouting had taken over the night, and I knew that even if they could hear me, no one would listen. Not tonight.

A distinct prickling sensation slid down my back, and I turned away from Kyle, scanning the crowd behind me. That's when I saw her. Head and shoulders above the rest of the crowd, a wild mess of dark hair tangled with strands of ivy, face like a model from one of the black-and-white arty shoots in *Vogue*, angular and inhuman, mind-blowing beauty. A Hidden girl with ivy in her hair: I knew there'd be more, that the Hidden would come in their hundreds. I grabbed Blue's arm, but then realized just how much I'd have to explain, and by that time a crowd from his drama class had caught up with us and I'd lost his attention again, for now, anyway.

The Hidden were here. They were among us. They were coming for us.

Joe. All I had to do was run through the woods back down to the Reach and find him. He'd faced the Hidden before –

he'd know what to do. Maybe Joe would even know how to find Lissy. She could deal with this – she'd hurled that creepy Hidden boy clear across the clearing. I felt cold inside just thinking about that, and couldn't even be sure what disturbed me the most: the memory of his cold hands on my skin, or Lissy's inhuman strength and her ruthlessness. *She's not dead, she's not dead.* The words spun crazily in my head, and I still couldn't make sense of them.

I grabbed Blue's arm again, tugging him away from Jessie and the drama lot for a moment. "Listen," I said, "I'm heading back to the house for a minute – be careful, right? And, Blue – I know everyone thinks I'm being crazy, but I really, really think you should go home. Please."

Blue gave me a look, half totally exasperated and half worried. "What's *wrong* with you tonight, Connie? Have you taken something?"

"No, I haven't taken anything. Listen. You're my oldest friend in Hopesay, Blue. We've been friends since my first week at school, when everyone else was too embarrassed to talk to me because my sister had just died. Just trust me. When have I ever lied or tried to bullshit you?"

He stared back – a weird, frightened understanding in his eyes. "Never."

"I never have and you know it." I tightened my grip on his arm till I could feel the lean cords of muscle beneath his lumberjack shirt, beneath his skin. He just stared at me, and I didn't look away. "Go home, Blue," I whispered. "Take the others, as many as you can, and get out of here. Please."

And it felt like a hundred years had passed with just Blue

and me staring at each other when Jessie appeared at his side, giving me a poisonous look. For once Blue paid her no attention at all.

"I'm going back to the Reach, OK?" I said, quietly, so that Jessie couldn't hear me above the music. "I need to find Joe. I'm serious, Blue. Take the others and get out of here."

Blue nodded, never taking his eyes away from mine. "OK, Connie. Listen, do you want someone to go with you?"

I shook my head. "I'll be OK. Just *go*."

I had to find Lissy, find Joe. I couldn't finish this alone. I pushed through the crowd away from Blue, praying that he'd be true to his word and wondering what Joe was even going to do about all this when I managed to wake him up. Had Dad bothered to stick around? Would he make the effort to see me in the morning? What could we do, anyway? With Dad and Joe on board there'd still only be three of us – I could see now that even Dad would struggle to get rid of this many people, no matter if he was a member of this ridiculous all-powerful Fontevrault group. I didn't like his chances of getting rid of the Hidden, either.

I was really having to force my way through the crowd now, and there were a lot of faces I didn't even recognize – kids had come out here from a hell of a lot further than Hopesay Edge. Just how far had the news about this party spread?

The further away I got from the main crowd, the more Hidden I saw – not many, hardly more than five or six, but enough that my heart rate shot up and cold, slick sweat spread across my back. They were so indistinct, hard at first to pick out from among the rest of the crowd: tall, slender interlopers. There was just something different about the poised way they held themselves, how they stood with the coiled-up strength of cats: *Hidden*. A good few minutes passed before I realized the handful of Hidden weren't just moving at random through the crowd.

They were herding us.

The Hidden were silently moving everyone in the woods closer together, gently urging the crowd into the clearing and no one except me had even noticed. I felt like the blood had just drained out of my body, right through my feet: we were in the presence of a higher intelligence. Maybe even a higher predator. Panicking, I turned to the first group of people I could see – I didn't even recognize them, and they looked way too old to be at school.

"The party's over." My voice was harsh with panic, and I knew I sounded crazy. "Look, we've all got to get out of here."

They stared at me like I'd just fallen out of the sky. One of the girls was wearing glasses with heavy black frames. "Right!" she laughed. "Thanks, hon, but we're fine."

"Look, I'm serious. It's time to go." I turned away, shouting at everyone I could see. "Time to go home, people. Come on, get out of here."

No one paid me the slightest bit of attention – all I got were a couple of weird looks, and then everyone turned back to whatever they were doing, tilting a bottle of red wine to drink the last dregs, leaning over to light someone else's cigarette, whispering into the ear of a friend.

One of the other girls smiled, a little more sympathetic than her buddy with the glasses. "Are you the kid whose party this is? I heard it was just some teenager. The best thing you can do now is just go with it and deal with the fallout later. Call the police and people are just going to get hurt, OK?"

I stared at her, breathing hard. I felt light-headed: terrified that I was going to pass out. "You don't understand. It's not safe here any more. There's – there's dangerous people here." I knew how paranoid that had to sound. No one was going to take me seriously spouting that kind of talk.

The girls exchanged glances, worried and obviously finding me hugely irritating at the same time. "Look, hon – where are your friends? Do you want us to help you find them?"

Helplessness washed over me. "Just go," I begged. "Just get out of here." I started running then, pelting through the woods towards the Reach, desperate to find Joe, knowing that the girls wouldn't run, that they hadn't listened. I'd led everyone into a huge trap.

I ran and ran through a gradually thinning crowd of teenagers all heading for the woods, for the trees, for the Hidden, without the smallest clue that they were being herded together like sheep – and for what purpose? I finally hurled myself down the path, ready to take the last stretch down to the Reach at a full-on sprint. When I reached that corner ahead, I'd be able to see the lights from the house, kitchen windows glowing like slabs of gold against the night.

But before I rounded the corner, a tall, slender shadow

melted away from the trees at the edge of the path, and my escape route was blocked. A Hidden boy stood before me, so beautiful in his ragged clothes: a moth-eaten fur pelt, torn white shirt, knee-high leather boots with jangling buckles. *Briar*. It was Briar – the one Lissy had torn away from me just hours earlier.

He smiled, so terrible and so beautiful. "Where are you going in such a rush, little girl? Lissy's not here now." And Briar stepped towards me slowly, deliberately, because now he had all the time in the world.

25

Joe

And I'm running down the lane, high hedges on either side, no way out, no escape. They're chasing me; I hear the heavy thud of their footfalls on tarmac, Fontevrault – *the Fontevrault want me because I know too much about the Hidden. I've seen too much, heard too much. I know the truth, just like David Creed knew the truth a hundred years ago, and they shot him—*

The dream shifts with a sudden jerk, and now my hands are tethered behind my back and everything is dark, rough fabric bound across my eyes: I'm blindfolded. I lean back against splintered wood. I'm tied to a post driven into the ground. I can't move. All I can do is wait for the bullet—

I woke with a jerk, curtains whipped by a wind that died down just seconds later. My heart was racing like I'd been running, and I was still wearing yesterday's clothes. I'd never meant to fall asleep. Always the same bloody dream – me in the place of David Creed the morning he was shot for desertion. I couldn't ever seem to shake it off. It'd been easy enough for the Fontevrault to have him falsely accused of desertion in 1917 just because he'd found out about the Hidden, easy enough for them to have him shot in the head. What the hell were the Fontevrault going to do now, to me and Connie a hundred years later, when they realized that the Gateway was open again? David Creed had been just one person. For all I knew, the Hidden were swarming all over Hopesay Edge. Everyone in the village might've seen them. Adam and Rafe might've thrown them a red herring with that story about one of the Hidden being spotted in India, but the Fontevrault didn't even trust Adam to begin with: he'd hidden the truth about Lissy, not his real daughter, for fourteen years.

They'll come to Hopesay. The Fontevrault will come. I squeezed my eyes shut, jolted back to the day they hunted us down six years ago, me and Rafe. Rafe's car screeching to a halt on a rain-sodden country lane just a few miles short of the Reach, a whisper short of smacking head-on into the van coming the other way. The Fontevrault men tumbling out, looking so ordinary, so boring, like a pair of estate agents in cheap suits. Knowing that Rafe couldn't run with his ankle smashed up. The way he'd looked at me. *Run, Joe.* They took him. They just took him—

I glanced up, drenched with sweat – my bedside clock shone red numbers at the ceiling: three thirty in the morning. I must have sat up so late, trying so hard not to bloody fall asleep that I'd never even got undressed. In the distance, sirens wailed – police – louder as their car got closer and closer – no their *cars*: plural. *Shit.* The Hidden? We were never going to keep this off the Fontevrault's radar. Not now. Then I heard music – the dull, low thud of a heavy bass line.

Music up in the woods and police. This had Connie's name all over it.

Idiot! I thought. *Idiot, idiot, idiot. You should've checked on her earlier.*

Swearing softly to myself, I got out of bed and pushed open the door, stepping out onto the landing, hitting the light switch. Ancient floorboards creaked beneath my feet and Miles's oil-painted ancestors stared at me from the walls, looking down their aristocratic noses like I was a thief.

"*Connie?*" I hissed outside her bedroom door. No answer. I pushed open the door, pausing on the threshold, trying to avoid setting foot inside Connie's private domain. "Con?"

I stepped over a heap of clothes spewing out of a chest of drawers, closer to the bed, a heap of duvets and blankets. Her bedroom window was jammed open with a book, curtains fluttering. And the bed was empty. A jolt of fear shot through me. I'd been in this place before years earlier – with Rafe. Breaking into Lissy's room to find her gone, nothing there but a pile of dead winter leaves, the calling card of the Hidden.

"What do you think you're doing?" Adam's voice was rough with anger as he stepped into the room. He must've been woken by the noise, too.

I turned around to face him, avoiding the temptation to point out I wasn't interested in violating his precious daughter. "She's not here." The words stuck in my throat.

Adam said nothing but just pushed past me tearing the heap of duvets and eiderdowns away from the mattress. There was nothing but the faint, warm scent of Connie herself.

"God," Adam said, as if he'd forgotten that I was even there. "Not again. Not again. Oh, please – not again." And I knew he was remembering Lissy disappearing as a baby, stolen by Larkspur on their father's command.

"There's no leaves," I pointed out. "No dead leaves. It's not the Hidden – not this time. She's gone off her own back. Can't you hear the music? It's some kind of party, way out of control—"

"Yes, with the Hidden everywhere. Damned idiots." Adam, already pale in the moonlight, lost all colour at that moment, and just looked dead. I wondered if he was remembering Connie's mother, Miriam – that party at the Reach, long ago when they weren't much older than me. Miriam came face to face with the Swan King, unable ever quite to leave him behind from that day on, her life chewed up and destroyed just as I'd wrecked my own obsessing over Lissy. Mortals and the Hidden just don't mix. Adam and me ran for the door.

26

Connie

Briar laughed, smiling at me, and I couldn't understand how someone so beautiful could also be so creepy and disgusting. I turned and hurled myself up the path back the way I'd come, sprinting uphill as fast as I could, screaming Joe's name and then Lissy's over and over again in the hope that one of them might hear me. I didn't once call for Dad. *Traitor. Liar. Liar.*

If the rest of the Hidden had gatecrashed my party, then where *was* Lissy? She was one of them. *Not-human, not-human, not-human.* And Briar was closer all the time as I crashed on through the trees – I heard snatches of laughter, even of song, and once I even felt the chilly jolt of a cold fingertip brushing the back of one arm, so teasing. He was letting me run, enjoying the chase.

I stopped and whirled around to look behind me, breathless with the effort of the run but mostly with sheer terror. I couldn't see Briar anywhere and I couldn't hear his footsteps behind me, but I could hear him laughing, his voice carried on a wind that was now picking up every second, shaking the branches above our heads, whipping at my long skirt, although the sound of his laughter seemed now to be coming from up ahead rather than the path curling back through the trees towards the Reach.

That was when I first heard the screaming – a girl's voice, high and ragged with panic and fear until her screams coalesced into one long sobbing wail, and I followed the sound, everyone else too wasted to take much notice, until the crowd thinned out completely and I was running alone through the trees. I should have known it was a huge mistake, just running towards the scream.

I could see her now – a girl pinned to the ground beneath one of the Hidden. With a horrible, dead-cold shock I realized it was Briar: that somehow he was ahead of me instead of behind, laughing and trying to tear off the girl's clothes, skirt up around her waist, white legs pale in the darkness, and it was clear what he wanted, what he was going to take. With one scream of pure rage, I lunged forwards and threw myself onto his back. Briar hissed with fury, whipping around with frightening, breathtaking strength, pinning me to the ground beside his victim – *Tia*, Tia who I sat next to in maths. She was frozen with terror and could only turn to look at me with wide, frightened eyes, her face stained with mud and tears, her lips forming soundless words.

"Leave. Her. Alone." I spat into the creature's catwalk-model face, but Briar only laughed and held me down with one hand, his cold fingers digging into my flesh once more.

"Two to enjoy now," he whispered, smiling. "So sweet."

I reached out with my free hand and scratched his eyes, yelling at Tia to run as he roared. I rolled over again to claw at his face. "Run!" I shrieked, and at last, at last I heard rapid footsteps, more voices crying out. Wrenching my head to one side, I saw a crowd of girls I recognized from Year Eleven snatching Tia away, their arms around her shoulders as she sobbed and sobbed, even as Briar pinned me to the ground once more. I'd bought Tia a few seconds to escape his grip but it was too late for me. I could hear the girls shouting, but Briar paid them no attention at all, nor the odd, silvery blood oozing from the scratch I'd torn into his eyelid. It was like he knew that there was absolutely nothing that they could do to help me, and so it was all just a joke to him.

"It's your turn now." Briar smiled, his face so close to mine I could feel the chill of his breath on my face. I spat at him, but he only laughed. "That's a pretty robe you're wearing, little maiden. Shall I take it off?"

With inhuman strength, he forced me onto my front, my face held down into the dirt, small twigs and stones pressing hard into my cheek. I could hear voices, someone shouting, people running – but all in the distance, all too far away. Had the girls who ran off with Tia gone to get help? Or was I on my own?

"*Connie! Connie!*" I heard a familiar voice calling my name, as if from a great distance, but I was so afraid that I couldn't make out who it was, or whether I was just so desperate for help my mind was playing tricks on me.

Briar didn't seem to notice a thing. I could just hear him breathing so slowly, feel his cold hands pressing down on my back, feel his fingers scrabbling for a way into my clothes. I heard the fabric of my skirt rip as he tore it away from my waist like a child ripping into her presents on Christmas Day, his gasp of fury as he realized I was wearing leggings as well. A sudden shock of cold shot through me as he pressed one hand against the small of my back, freezing fingers grappling inside the waistband of my leggings, my underwear, and I writhed away from his touch, mouth wide open in a silent scream, my face jammed hard against dirt and stones, dry dead leaves in my mouth, in my eyes. The woodland burst with the sound of my screaming; black tree trunks like spears against the moonlit sky, black leaves shaking in the wind, high above me but out of reach.

Briar just smiled down at me, his teeth shining white in the silvery light. "I'd forgotten how much I like it when mortal girls struggle." He reached for my top, pulling it up, laughing and trying to touch me. No matter how hard I struggled or kicked, I couldn't move him; he was so, so strong, stronger than iron. Stronger than stone. And all the time I was sobbing with fear and horror, and there was such a storm of voices and shouting in the woods that I couldn't make out what was happening at all.

And then just as I thought that there was no way out, and a cold, deep hopelessness washed over me, Briar was jerked away from me – not completely, just enough to loosen his grip on my clothes, and I looked up into the face of my dad, contorted with fury as he roared at the Hidden boy to get away from me, hauling at the filthy folds of his clothes with hands like claws.

"Connie, run!" Dad yelled, his voice bloody with rage,

and as I watched, the Hidden boy's face twisted with anger and again with that terrifying inhuman strength he turned on my father and closed both hands around his throat, picking him up as if he weighed no more than a baby, even as Dad gasped and clutched at the white cold hands at his neck, just hurling him away. I rolled away from Briar's grasp and looked up to see Dad slam with ferocious speed into the trunk of a tree just metres away, then drop to the ground. He lay still, his head at an odd angle, looking my way with blank, unseeing eyes, and I knew straight away that he was dead, that he'd died trying to save me.

My dad was dead. He'd been killed, and it was my fault, and the last time we'd spoken I'd screamed at him that he was a liar, a cheat, and that I never wanted to see him again. *My dad.* I dropped to my knees, and the flurry of dead leaves that flew up around me as I hit the earth seemed to take for ever to drift back down, as if time had actually slowed.

Briar turned back to me, his white teeth shining in the moonlight again as he smiled. I'd lost my chance to run away. He was an animal. Not-human, not-human. He leaned so close I could feel the chill of his breath on my face – cold, not like human breath. The frozen hopelessness washed over me again, and I knew there was no point in fighting any more.

"*You're mine now.*" Reaching out, his hand slid down my belly, taking his time, knowing there was nothing I could do – and then he stopped, he just stopped, and for some reason he wasn't touching me any more. I scrambled up but found my legs wouldn't support me. I turned to see Briar backing slowly away through the trees, utterly soundless, treading in total silence across last year's dead leaves. *Dad?* I thought, burning with the ridiculous hope that he wasn't really dead, that he'd somehow struggled to his feet and found a way of forcing Briar to retreat. But Dad lay on the ground just metres away, watching me with dead eyes. He was gone; he was just gone…

Lissy, then. Had I found her, at last? Heart hammering, I turned, expecting to see my sister in her cloak of golden feathers, praying against all hope that she'd come to find me. But Lissy wasn't there, either. There was only a boy I'd never seen before. He stood silently, just paces away – tall like the Hidden, but olive-skinned and slightly older, somehow, ragged dark hair hanging in his eyes. And he was holding a bow and arrow, the bowstring pulled back taut. There was something so still about him that he seemed to make the rest of the world slow down, too. Shaking, I glanced back over my shoulder at Briar – *Dad's murderer* – who was still backing away, step by step, staring at the newcomer.

"*You?*" Briar whispered at the boy. "Nicolas de Mercadier." His voice shook with mockery. "So, the traitor has returned." I was completely forgotten now, discarded on the ground like a piece of rubbish. "Now the Hidden are free, you have returned. And yet, it was always in your power to free us, to open the Gateway, and you did not."

The newcomer didn't move – *Nicolas?* – the bowstring was still pulled back tight, brushing against his ear. His gaze flickered towards me, then back to Briar, but he said nothing, waiting. Nicolas was motionless except for the gentle rise and fall of his chest. I looked away, staring at Dad's body, unable to believe what had just happened, that he was really dead. We were alone in the clearing.

Briar smiled with sheer malice, nodding at the arrowhead aimed at his heart. "Would you really do it, traitor? Would you kill me with iron?"

Traitor?

"Don't try me." Holding the bow absolutely rigid, the boy he'd called Nicolas spoke with a light accent that I couldn't place.

And slowly, slowly, my father's murderer backed away until finally he turned and just ran off through the trees without a sound, without so much as the crack of a twig, slipping away through the trees like a shadow. Breathless, I scrambled up the second he'd gone, rushing over to where Dad's body lay on the floor, his head still at that horrible awkward angle. His neck must've broken, either when the creature grabbed him by the throat or when he landed.

I crouched at his side, staring down into his face, shaking and shaking and shaking and shaking. It was so strange – Dad still looked like Dad, his face was still almost the same, his mouth slack and slightly open, a trickle of blood seeping from one corner, but at the same time my dad wasn't there. He was gone. I was never going to see him or speak to him again. Tears streamed down my face, and I knew they'd never stop. My heart was still racing – what would Briar have done to me if this Nicolas guy hadn't turned up? I knew I'd be able to feel the chill of Briar's hands on my skin every night before I went to sleep, that it would haunt me for ever.

"You can't help the dead." Nicolas had lowered his bow and stood watching me in complete silence, waiting. There was something about the way he looked at my face that made me uneasy, like he'd just recognized me from somewhere, and yet I was certain I'd never seen him before in my life. "Get up," he said, quietly. "The Hidden are hunting this night, now that they're free. It's not safe."

"My dad." I sounded breathless, airless. "He killed my dad." I clutched my torn clothes around me. My skirt was ripped beyond repair, trampled into the dirt. *The Hidden are hunting?* What did that even mean? What had I done, opening that Gateway, moving that stupid iron cross? "It's all my fault," I whispered, wrapping my arms around myself, shuddering uncontrollably. My eyes felt burning hot like I was going to cry, but I didn't. I couldn't.

"You need to get away from here. Get up." Nicolas reached out, offering me one slim, sun-browned hand, but I flinched away, not wanting to touch anyone or anything. He didn't force it, but just waited for me to scramble to my feet.

"I can't just leave him here. He's my father." I got up with one quick step backwards, never taking my eyes away from Nicolas's face. He really did look Hidden, tall and with that cold, frightening beauty, but there was something different about him, too – his skin was much darker, tanned by the sun when all the others I'd seen were so pale, the skin around his eyes faintly seamed with fine lines, even though he looked so young. "Are you one of the Hidden? Why should I trust you? You look like one of them." My voice was cracked and thin.

"Listen, I can get you out of here safely but you'll have to trust me." Nicolas paused, waiting, avoiding my question like a politician. He held up the arrow, holding my gaze over the shining arrowhead. "This is finest steel: it's full of iron and the Hidden know it'll kill them. Iron's the only thing that *will* kill them – they don't grow old; they can't die unless their blood is poisoned with iron. If you want to get out of here without being mauled, then come with me. The Hidden have been imprisoned a long time, and now the Swan King's dead, they think they're safe to wander, to take what they will from the mortals. Your father's gone; there's no helping him now. He's nothing but earth and worms. Would he want you to put yourself in danger for his sake?"

I couldn't move. *Earth and worms?* I couldn't speak. I was just frozen with shock.

In the distance, I heard the faint wail of sirens and realized that the pounding bass line that had been reverberating through the woods for hours had now fallen silent. *Party's over.* Nicolas expertly slipped the arrow into a pouch strapped to his back and shouldered the bow like a rucksack. Without another word, he just started walking off through the trees, and all the time, the police sirens were louder and louder – I could hear more shouting now, too. I felt like I was watching myself in a film, the party destroyed around me with a soundtrack of crashing vegetation as people ran off through the trees, the night torn up with the sound of desperate crying. Even though Briar was long gone, I could still feel the touch of his cold, cold hands on my skin, and if that Nicolas boy had a weapon they were afraid of, I would follow him and take it for myself.

I'd find the creature who had killed my father, and I would make him pay before the night was over.

27

Nicolas de Mercadier

It doesn't take Connie long to catch me up: she's nobody's fool. I'm armed and she's not, and the Hidden are hungry for mortal girls – and mortal boys, too. I don't look round but I can tell she's still shaking like a sapling in a gale; her breathing is harsh and ragged, and I can hear the beat of her heart.

Connie Harker. I'd recognize that face anywhere – God knows, I've seen it in place of my own reflection every day for weeks. I've just saved the life of the girl I came here to kill. A wave of sheer rage rolls through me: because of this girl and her idiot of a sister, the Swan King is dead, the closest I've ever had to a real father gone to dust. It would have been so easy to let loose that arrow. What in Hell's name stopped me spoiling Briar's fun and just killing her? Or I could have killed her afterwards, but the way she crouched by her father's corpse like that, just staring at it— The Swan King is dead, and I'll never see him again; I'll never get the chance to beg his forgiveness for not setting the Hidden free. The truth is Connie and I are one and the same, twinned by our sorrow, our grief. I'm worse than Larkspur. What am I going to do with her now?

"I can hear police sirens. They're coming." Her voice is still shaking, her clothes in disarray. "Look, what's going to happen when the police arrive and see all those things? Those Hidden?" She laughs, a brittle, glass-like sound. "And why do you carry a bow and arrow?" She stares with incredulous horror at the bow and quiver strung up to my shoulder, as if she is unable to quite believe what's right before her eyes. She lifts her gaze to my face and stares right back at me without a trace of visible fear, even though she's just almost been ravaged and her father has been killed before her eyes. Despite the misery she's caused, and despite the knowledge that I'm planning to murder Connie as her sister watches, I can't help admiring her nerve.

My voice is rough, harsh. "I can hold off one or two of them but the Hidden are hungry, and they've been waiting a long time. I don't want to kill them all. Come on, you need to get out of here." I can decide how to dispose of her later.

Lissy Harker will pay for that golden cloak that she wears. I will make her weep her eyes dry over every last feather.

Lissy

"We now face a war." I speak in a cold, low hiss, but I know all the Hidden hear every last word, a scattered tribe gathered in the graveyard, huddled amongst a thicket of ancient yews far older than the mortal church casting a shadow over us. "Could you not control yourselves for just one night?" I demand, shaking with rage I can hardly control – I want to hurt them all, to punish. "The mortals won't forgive their young ones being hurt. Do you want your freedom, or to dwindle and die out till there are no Hidden left at all?"

The Hidden cower in silence, hundreds of pairs of gunmetal-silver eyes glittering in the darkness, all too afraid to reply. And no matter how much I hated my father when he was alive, nothing can stop me longing for him to be here now. He would know what to do. Hidden and mortals dancing in the woods: I know that this can only end in sorrow, just as it has always done.

Connie

The old gatehouse sat alone in the trees, overgrown with a tangle of dark green ivy, windows boarded up, the front door scratched and battered. Behind us, the woods were full of shouting policemen and screaming teenagers. Once, there'd been five different driveways leading all the way from the main road to the Reach, but the gatehouse hadn't been lived in for years, the old driveway long since abandoned.

"How do we get in?" Nicolas's eyes flickered around the gatehouse and the tangle of trees growing right up to the front door.

"Around the back." I didn't want to go inside with him: even though Briar was long gone, I felt the chill of his hands on my body; I couldn't stop shaking. Dad was dead. I was never going to see him again, his corpse just left behind in the woods to rot like a piece of meat.

Nicolas glanced at me, calculating. "You go in, I'll guard the door. I'll stay outside." He held back a tangled stream of brambles for me to duck under, and there was something reassuring in the way he stepped back to let me past. He was making it clear that he wouldn't try to touch me, and so I trusted him just a little – just enough to use him for protection. After all, I had no one else, and Nicolas had a weapon that would kill Briar: *iron would kill them.* I cradled the knowledge deep inside myself, and it made me want to smile.

"No. Come in." I turned back to look at Nicolas, towering above me and holding the strands of bramble back with his bare hands as if they didn't hurt him at all, the bow and arrow strapped to his shoulder like he was a hero from an old legend.

The woods were exploding with panic and noise now, screaming, people running, crashing through low-hanging branches, even a dog barking, but Nicolas was so still he made it seem that all this was happening somewhere so far away that it didn't matter.

"Are you sure? I can guard the door from out here."

In answer, I just pushed through the overgrown tangle of bracken and dog rose till at last we reached the back door, and I went into the tumbledown kitchen. I was so tired that I could hardly even move. My vision blurred, and I stumbled on the doorstep, and Nicolas reached out and steadied me, the touch of his long, suntanned fingers surprisingly cool against my skin. I flinched at his touch, trying to push away memories of Briar.

"You should rest. We'll do well enough here for a while till the madness out there dies down a little." There was something so old-fashioned about the way he spoke. He stepped silently across the torn-up lino floor, eyes flickering past a row of kitchen cupboards, one with the door torn off:

a heap of empty Coke cans on the rotting sideboard. I stared at him, unable to forget the way Briar had pushed me to the ground ready to do whatever he wanted. The truth was I was too scared to let my guard down. It wasn't safe to sleep.

If that's what the Hidden boys are like, I couldn't help thinking, *then what does that mean about Lissy? Is she evil, too?*

Lissy wasn't dead. Everyone had lied to me. I couldn't trust anyone.

Nicolas stared back as if he'd just read my mind. "I'm not like Briar, all right? Mortal girls like you don't exactly hold that much appeal."

Unsmiling, he followed me through the kitchen into a sitting room littered with ashtrays and old magazines. I'd spent pretty much every night out here with Blue, Kyle and the others last half-term, but that was weeks ago now. It felt like a different lifetime, those nights spent drinking Coke spiked with stolen wine and watching Jessie doing tarot readings, as if all that had happened to someone else.

If I hadn't been in the woods at night, Dad would never have come looking for me. I may as well just have killed him with my own bare hands. It was my fault. My head churned and I couldn't hold on to a single train of thought for more than a few seconds. *There are people who look almost human, but they're not human.* And they were everywhere.

"How do you know so much about all this, anyway?" My voice shook as I sank down into the battered old sofa. The cushions stank of stale red wine.

Nicolas stood leaning in the doorway, watching me with disinterest. "Because I'm both, that's why. I'm Hidden and mortal, just like your sister. Get some rest."

He knew about Lissy?

"How do you know about my sister?" Why was I always the last to find out?

Nicolas smiled then, and it lit up his face, and suddenly he was so bright and beautiful, so completely different that I felt my misery lift by just the tiniest of fractions. "Go to sleep, little mortal girl." And that was the only answer he would give me. The last I remembered before sleep came rolling in as I lay curled up on the sofa was Nicolas standing by the window, watching through the smeared cobwebby glass and overhanging tangles of ivy, almost like he was watching over me. Sleep swept over me in unstoppable waves, drawing me down into the deep darkness. I didn't know Nicolas, and he didn't know me, but he'd cared enough to stop Briar, and he cared enough to keep watch as I slept, which was far more than anyone else did. He was a stranger, but he was all I had.

30

Joe

I hurled myself through the trees, dodging the running, panicking kids all around me. Was it the Hidden they were so afraid of, or just the sirens getting louder and louder? *"Connie!"* I'd shouted her name so many times my voice was raw and ragged. The trees thinned out, and there was no one here except some guy lying crumpled at the foot of a huge oak. Hammered, probably. "Shit," I whispered, and even though every instinct was telling me to run like hell and get to Connie before the Hidden found her, even though doing that was worse than looking for a needle in a bloody haystack, even so, I couldn't stop myself walking slowly across the clearing to the drunken loser slumped on the ground. The least I could do was give him a shake, tell him to get home. He lay facing away from me, wrapped in a dark coat, pale hair standing out against the muck he was sprawled in, one arm flung out behind him at an odd angle. The coat was weird. I'd been to a lot of parties like this, out in the woods or up the side of a fell somewhere, and you didn't exactly see people in sensible outdoor wear.

And as I stepped closer, my feet crunching through last

winter's dead leaves, I realized that the hair wasn't just fair but actually grey, and that I recognized the coat: the waterproof jacket I'd seen Adam grab as we ran out of the back door just hours earlier.

Even as I called his name, I don't think I really expected him to answer. I stepped closer and closer, knowing what I was going to see even before I looked down at Adam's dead face, at the small trickle of blood emerging from the corner of his mouth. Kneeling at his side, I brushed one hand over Adam's eyes, closing the lids. But even as I did that, I couldn't resist following the direction he'd last been looking in. And there in the leaves I saw something glittering.

Getting to my feet, I forced myself to walk across the carpet of leaf-mulch and dry twigs till I was standing right above a swathe of shiny silver fabric, tangled and trodden into the leaves. Connie's skirt, the one she'd worn that awful Christmas Eve, months before.

"Connie." I whispered her name, reaching into my back pocket for my phone. But as I crouched down beside the torn remains of her skirt, I saw why she hadn't answered any of my increasingly desperate messages. Her phone lay just an arm's length away, instantly recognizable as Connie's, covered in stickers, the screen now shattered.

Connie wasn't just gone, she was unreachable.

31

Connie

—And I see the face of a boy who looks just like Lissy, just like my sister — the same tangled red hair and pale beauty. Larkspur. It's funny — now I know who they both really are, I see echoes of the Swan King, the boy who haunted my dreams for so long. Except he wasn't a boy: he was a king, a powerful, merciless king. Larkspur's looking right at me; it's as if I've glanced into a mirror and he has stolen my reflection, replacing it with his own like a cuckoo chick pushing little sparrows out of the nest. And his face is wet with tears—

I woke with a dull ache in my neck, sprawled awkwardly on the sofa, taking a good few seconds to regain my bearings. Early-morning sunlight streamed in through the filthy window: I was in the gatehouse. With Nicolas. My head was thick with agony — it hurt even to open my eyes. I'd been dreaming. Again. I was no longer in control of my own mind — I couldn't stop it parting company with my body, travelling to strange and dangerous places, to the Hidden.

Get a grip, Connie.

Dad was dead in the woods. Flies would be landing on him, beetles crawling over him… *Nicolas.* I turned, shifting onto my side – a coat had been spread out over me, soft folds of worn-in leather that smelled faintly of warm grass. At the sound of running water, I rolled over to face the door leading into the kitchen, the headache jabbing deeper into my skull every time I moved. I rubbed my eyes, my vision shaking as the headache pulsed. Nicolas stood at the sink with his back to me, leaning forwards to splash his face with water, dark hair curled about the nape of his neck. He wore a loose white shirt, and as I watched, he pulled it off over his head, letting it fall to the cracked lino tiles, washing his arms and his body, sending shining trails of water down his back. His body was long and lean and his shoulder blades jutted out like little wings.

I stared, massaging my throbbing temples and wishing like hell that I was carrying aspirin. Was it my blurred vision or was there something wrong with Nicolas's back? I rubbed my eyes, trying to push away the jabbing pain: the skin was ridged all the way down to his waist, ridged and marked with faint silvery lines, like old scars. I couldn't stop staring, even though I knew it was wrong, and I would find it seriously freaky if anyone watched me in the same way.

"Seen enough now?" Nicolas turned to look at me as he stooped to pick up the shirt and my face burned. He slid his shirt back on, his expression completely unreadable, before turning back to the sink to splash his face with water once more.

"What happened to you?" I asked, since he'd just called me out for staring. There was no point in pretending I hadn't seen. "Are they scars?" The second I spoke, I was kicking myself for being so blatant and unsubtle, but Nicolas didn't seem to care. He just filled a couple of ancient brown mugs with water and walked into the sitting room, dropping into the old armchair.

"Put it this way, mortal girl, when I was your age things were different. My stepfather and I were not the best of friends."

"Did he use to hit you? That's so wrong." I couldn't get that image of those scars out of my mind. And *hit* wasn't even close to a strong enough word. Those marks hadn't been left by someone's hand. They'd been left by a weapon. "You had to live with someone who did that? It's abuse. Your stepfather should've been sent to prison."

"But he *was* the law." Nicolas gave me this beautiful incredulous smile, as if he were laughing at me for being so concerned, and passed over one of the mugs of water. "It was just the way things were – take a step wrong and you'd get a whipping. But even for those days my stepfather was a hard man. I used to think that one day he'd go too far, that one day I'd just bleed to death." He smiled again. "But I was wrong about that. I had a wild temper then. I used to like making him rage. He looked so stupid when he did it."

"Well, your stepfather had no right to leave scars like that, whatever you'd done." I held on to the mug with both hands, unable to forget those pale silvery marks, the damage that must have been done for the shadows of them to still be visible. I swallowed, trying to ignore the headache. Surely it hadn't been acceptable for parents to hit their kids with whips for a long time – a hundred years

211

at least? And what had Nicolas meant when he laughed and said, *But he was the law.* As if violence like that was nothing unusual. Seconds passed by in silence before I dared ask the question: "When you say it was a long time ago, how long exactly do you mean?"

"Is that really important?"

I took a sip of water – it tasted almost earthy, like the pipes had been corrupted with something, but I started to feel a little more human. "It matters to me. Look – there's so much I've seen and heard over the last two days that makes no sense at all. I've seen things I never thought were possible – these creatures, these Hidden, and my sister is one of them. I thought she was dead – my own parents told me she was dead and she's not. Everyone's been lying to me for years. Have you any idea how that feels? I just don't know what to believe any more. Give me the facts so I know exactly what I'm dealing with. Why did you save me from that Hidden boy in the woods? How old are you?"

Nicolas set his cup down on the stained brown and orange carpet, then leaned back in his armchair, dark hair falling away from his face as I watched him, long eyelashes lowered, brushing his cheekbone. "Do you really want to know?"

"*Yes.*"

"Very well, then. I was born more than eight centuries ago. My mother was the richest heiress in Europe, and before she was even married for the first time, her father sent her to the mouth of the cave at L'Anse aux Audes, riding on a white mare with cloth of gold spread over the saddle and lilac petals strewn all through her hair, like a hound bitch left tied out to a stake for the wolves."

I stared at him. He had to be making this up. But even as the thought drifted across my mind, I knew that he wasn't. He was telling the truth. "*Eight centuries ago?*" The day before yesterday, I would have laughed at this conversation. Not now.

Nicolas shrugged. "It's a long time, Connie, to walk the earth alone. My mother was mated to one of the Hidden – the Swan King's right-hand man. He was murdered not long afterwards – some say on the orders of my mortal grandfather, who was a powerful duke, the richest man in Christendom at the time. He didn't want anyone else to lay claim to his immortal grandchild – and more than anything else, he wanted an immortal heir. My mother was fourteen years old, just like you. And when her father, the duke, kept Christmas that year at the great abbey at Fontevrault, I was born. And I survived, and I was concealed there as my mother was married off first to the King of France, then to Henry of Anjou, who inherited the English throne. Children of mortals and Hidden usually die, poisoned by their own blood. But I survived, and now, such a long time later, so has your sister." He smiled. "The Fontevrault have always been so terrified of interbreeding, but it's not exactly easy to achieve."

"OK. So you're like this hybrid. You and Lissy. OK. I get that now. You're eight hundred years old. Fine, fine." I half wanted to laugh – it was all so crazy. "OK. OK. Since you're the one with all the answers, why did I keep seeing that boy – the Swan King?" I still saw him in the back of my mind, that shining black hair tangled in the white feathers of his cloak.

Nicolas looks at me over the rim of his cup, leaning back against the armchair. "Because you're Tainted, and because he wanted to escape, and he used you."

"*Tainted?* What's that supposed to mean? That's a horrible word – it makes me sound dirty."

"You remember being ill? When you were a child?"

"Yeah. I was still in hospital when Lissy died –" I broke off, staring at him – "when Lissy disappeared. That must have been when she went to live with the Hidden."

"When the Swan King claimed her, yes. He was Lissy's father, Connie… She killed her own father."

I watch him, uneasy. There was something different in Nicolas's tone then – an edge of hardness that sent a cold sliver of fear down my back. I couldn't get my head around it: my sister was a murderer. Nicolas just went on as if nothing had happened, and I was desperate enough for the truth that all I could do was listen. "When Lissy was born and she survived, Larkspur was ordered by his father to bring her home to the Hidden. Their father was the boy you saw, Connie, the one who kept appearing in your dreams, who told you to open the Gateway. The Swan King. Larkspur disobeyed, though, and returned Lissy to Miriam – to your mother – just a few days later. The Swan King granted them fourteen years together, though, but you and your brother were cursed to die unless Lissy was returned to the Hidden at the allotted time."

"Mum had to choose between us?" The horror of it

214

washed over me. No wonder she hated me.

"Your parents had no choice. You were cursed with a Hidden sickness as a reminder to her not to try and cheat her way out of the bargain, and if it wasn't for Larkspur, you would have died in that hospital, Connie, six years ago. There is no mortal medicine that could have saved you."

"So the Hidden cheated, in the end. They were going to kill me anyway." I shivered thinking of the tall and beautiful red-headed boy, Lissy's brother: Larkspur. He'd saved my life. "I don't understand what this has to do with why I kept seeing the Swan King in my Dream – it was like he'd got through to me somehow, like we were really communicating. I used to dream about Lissy all the time, too. Like just now."

Nicolas glanced out of the window. "When Larkspur healed you, you became Tainted – joined to the Hidden world. That's why you dream about your sister, and it's how the Swan King was able to reach you. The barrier between the Halls of the Hidden and the mortal world is thin here, so close to the Gateway. You saw through it, Connie. You still could now, if you chose. You're bound to the Hidden, like it or not." He smiled. "Think of it as a unique ability. You can travel between two worlds in your dreams. How many people can say that?"

I stared at him. "But what if I don't want to be Tainted? I don't want to be part of this at all, and I definitely don't want anything to do with those things – those creatures. They're evil. You saw what he was trying to do to me, that thing in the woods." I knew I'd wake up years from now still feeling the chill of Briar's hands groping my flesh, still remembering my dad lying with his eyes wide open and his head at that horrible, wrong angle like he was just a broken doll.

"Not all of the Hidden would have done the same — Larkspur for one. Think about it: are all mortals tyrants? The Hidden had been trapped for so long, Connie. The Gateway has been opened before, but none would have risked conduct like that whilst the Swan King still lived."

I stared down into my empty mug, fixing my eyes on the ring of tea stains. I couldn't help thinking about the pattern of silver scars running the length of Nicolas's back. Clearly I wasn't the only person in the room with a screwed-up family. "How did you get away from your stepfather, then? Didn't he try to find you?" Would Mum make any effort to look for me if one day I just never came home? She wouldn't even notice I'd gone. "You must have left at some point. How?"

Nicolas leaned forwards, his forehead resting on the window, facing away from me. "I was lucky. I had help." He was completely still again, and for a moment it was like he'd forgotten I was there: he'd just gone back to some other time, some other place. He pushed away from the window, turning to face me again. "Anyway. That's not important, not any more. What's the use in going over what has passed? Listen, the Swan King is dead, but who is the most powerful amongst all the Hidden now? Who can call them to order?" Nicolas asked, leaning back against the window frame, watching me with his dark eyes. Eight hundred years. He must have seen so much. "Your sister, Connie. You need Lissy. You need her now. Call her. Only she can help you to end this before any more harm is done."

"I can't—"

"You've already released the Hidden – you opened the Gateway. You saw what was happening in the woods. Your father is dead, and the Hidden are hungry for mortals – their warmth, for the children they can't bear. They can't help themselves. The mortals will destroy them in revenge. All it takes is an iron weapon – a whole race could be destroyed in the space of a few hours with just a couple of rounds of ammunition. Haven't you done enough damage?"

"I know it's my fault that thing killed my dad, OK? You don't need to keep reminding me. I don't care what happens to the Hidden, though. I wish they would all be destroyed with whatever weapon will do it." I squeezed my eyes shut, desperate to push away the memory of that Hidden boy pressing me down, soil and dead leaves in my mouth; trying to forget that I'd left my own father's dead body lying by a tree in the woods.

Nicolas stared at me. "Then you're as good as a murderer, Connie. Most of the Hidden have done nothing wrong. All they want is their freedom. If you refuse to call your sister, you may as well kill them all with your own hands."

"I can't call Lissy. I don't know how."

"Then try." Nicolas shoved himself away from the window and came to lean against the arm of the sofa, looking down at me. "Pretend that I'm Lissy: talk to me, Connie. Try. Do you want to let it all get worse and worse till everyone's dead? Are you some kind of coward, or are you going to take control? You're Tainted – use the power you have been given."

Nicolas was right. So much of this was my fault. If Lissy

could put a stop to it, and I had the ability to call her, then I had to try. I fixed my eyes on him, and I thought of Lissy. I thought of my sister, I held her picture in my mind – that endless red hair, her smile, that cloak of golden feathers – and I called her to me. And all the time Nicolas was smiling.

32

Lissy

We huddle in the shelter of the churchyard yews – hundreds of Hidden, all pressed together, clutching at one another's ragged finery as we listen to rain splashing from the branches into the puddles forming at our feet, and the heavy, repetitive thud of mortal footfalls. Someone is coming, and all I can do is hope that Larkspur was right, and that the ancient trees really will offer us a measure of concealment.

What must we do, O Queen? The Hidden are silent, their eyes wide with fear, their bone-white faces streaming with rain, but their thoughts drift across my mind like strands of cloud across a darkening sky. *O Queen, we are afraid, afraid of their mortal rage, their mortal iron. They would destroy all of us so easily with their weapons of iron—*

Wait. I tell them. *We are concealed, therefore do not be afraid.*

And even as I send the thought into the minds of my terrified people, a mortal boy bursts out of the trees and hurls himself over the stile into the churchyard. I recognize him immediately – that ragged hair swept back from his face. Joe. He stops, skidding in wet grass, and a fine spray of mud hits the Hidden closest to him. They shrink away, drawing their drenched and ragged silken cloaks closer about their shoulders.

Don't move! I order. *Silence.* I can't see how this is going to work. It's never going to work.

Joe stops, staring around the churchyard with wide, terrified eyes, pausing to wipe the rain from his face, but his gaze passes over us – a crowd of hundreds. Larkspur was right. Our father was right. The yews have saved us, the ancient, powerful yews, and Joe just runs on towards the village, his shoulders hunched against the rain.

Oh, Joe. I long to stop him, to ask what he is so afraid of, but my duty is to protect the Hidden, to hide them even from the one mortal I would trust with my sister's life. And as I look down at the puddle gathering at my feet in the pitted, rough grass of the churchyard, I see that it no longer reflects the furious grey sky above.

Lissy? I hear Connie's voice, just as loud as if she were standing right beside me.

I see her face in the water…

33

Joe

Adam was dead in the woods, his eyes just staring at nothing but Connie's torn-up clothes. He was dead, and I was on my own. How long would it be before the Fontevrault turned up in Hopesay? I sprinted down the high street past the butcher, trying to shake off that creepy feeling that I'd been watched, that someone other than me had been in the churchyard. *Watching.* I had to find Connie. I couldn't shake off the memory of finding the tattered rags of her skirt.

Don't be a bloody idiot, jumping at bloody shadows just because you've seen a dead body. Just find her.

Hopesay Edge was quiet, creepy: the usual row of dusty pick-up trucks and knackered Land Rovers parked up on the pavement just wasn't there. *They've found out about the party. Everyone's up at the Reach, looking for their kids.* I turned off the high street, tearing down the lane towards that cottage where me and Dad had once dropped off Connie, praying I'd got the right place because it'd been years and years since I was last in the village – the lane was just a rutted track, mud laced together with tufts of long dry grass. Finally, I recognized the black-and-white timbered cottage at the end and threw myself at the front door, banging on the glossy blue paint with both fists.

There was no reply, and I paced around to the kitchen window, peering in. I could hear a TV turned down low. "Connie!" I yelled. "Are you in there?" There was definitely someone at home. I thumped the door again and this time it opened, on a chain.

"She's not here. What do you want?" The kid looked like he hadn't slept. What was his name? Something weird and hippyish? *Blue.* And he looked very, very scared, his eyes darting around, trying to see if there was someone behind me. "Mum told me not to let anyone in."

She's not here. All that could mean was that Connie was either at the Reach – or still up in the woods. With the Hidden. *Nice work, Joe. Once again, you've run in the wrong bloody direction at the wrong time.* Despair washed over me. "I'm Joe, Connie's stepbrother. I thought Connie might be with you – I was hoping she might be with you."

Blue shook his head, lifting the chain and stepping back to let me in. He closed the door behind us, and the house smelled of spices and washing powder, homely and safe. "Listen, OK? There were these weird, strange people just everywhere, up in the woods, all over our party, and they weren't *right.* Connie knew. She made me promise to leave, but I shouldn't've let her go on her own. She said she was looking for you—" He broke off, obviously on the edge of complete panic. I remembered that feeling – that slow and terrifying realization that those things he'd seen were inhuman. That they were something else. And Connie wasn't with him.

"I haven't seen her. She didn't find me." I wasn't about to tell him I'd found Connie's dad dead, her ripped clothes scattered all over the clearing and no sign of her. *You idiot!* I wanted to shriek in his face. *Why the bloody hell did you let her go off on her own?*

Blue shook his head, as if I'd asked the question out loud. "I didn't know what she was on about. I thought she was going crazy – I hadn't seen them then. Those things. I hadn't— Look, you really don't know what's going on, do you?" He looked haunted, massive dark circles beneath his eyes.

Fear clenched my gut. "What?"

"Mika," Blue said, and his voice shook. "My sister's baby. They woke up this morning and he wasn't there. Everyone's out looking for him. I mean, Mika's just this tiny little baby – he can't survive without Amy." Blue paused, staring at me. "You know what the weirdest thing was? She came running in from the caravan first thing this morning; she was screaming, with all these leaves in her hands – dead leaves, everywhere. She said his cot was just full of dead leaves. So now Mika's gone as well as Connie."

I opened my mouth to speak but I couldn't. The police wouldn't find him. No one would find that baby now. He was with the Hidden. It was all starting again, the same story, all over again – a mortal child, stolen. On and on it would go, this nightmare, without end, till there was nothing left.

I turned and walked down the lane, listening to the dull click as Blue closed the front door behind me, the tiny metallic jingle as he hung the chain, as if that could possibly keep out the Hidden. And then, as I watched, a black SUV pulled up across the end of the lane, right onto the pavement, blocking my way back to the deserted high street of Hopesay Edge. I stood, waiting, as the engine died. The windows were darkened; the driver and any passengers all concealed.

Fontevrault. For a second, I closed my eyes in the mad hope the SUV would just disappear – it didn't. *It's just another dream. A waking dream. Get a grip, Joe.* When I opened them, the SUV was still there, real and black and shining like a seal on a rock, blocking the end of the lane. A huge, crushing weight settled on my shoulders, and I felt like I was being forced downwards into the earth at my feet.

"Good morning, Joe." An unfamiliar adult voice: *Fontevrault.* The speaker was behind me. They must've come down the tiny, rutted pathway that led around to the back of the Creeds' cottage at the end of the lane.

Without turning to look, I let the truth sink in. There were rows of terraced cottages on either side, with no way past. The Fontevrault had returned to Hopesay Edge as I'd always known they would, and this time, they'd found me.

34

Nicolas de Mercadier

Connie backs away, staring at me, her face white with shock. Her hands shake as if she has the palsy. "I did it. I saw Lissy, but I'm awake."

I smile, so very encouraging, trying not to let her see how impressed I am. I'm going to make Lissy Harker pay. "You've done well. You're Tainted and you're learning to control your power."

She glances at me with her green-glass eyes. So scornful. "Power? Like in a fairy tale?"

"Isn't this a fairy tale?" I can't help wanting to laugh – she's so tough and so ridiculously young and stupid. It's going to be a lot harder to kill her than I thought. "Come on. You'll need to eat, you need to stay strong and try again later. It's quieter out there now. I'm going to bring you a rabbit."

Connie makes a face. "I don't want to eat a rabbit." She stands up, and I can't help but notice how her fingers are still shaking and how she grabs hold of the chaise to stop them. "I'm coming with you."

"Do you really want to run into more of the Hidden?"

She stands, tilting her head up to look at me, and her

green eyes catch the light coming in through the window and look gold. "Right. And do you really think I want to stay here by myself?"

"Do it anyway." I need Connie Harker where I can find her. And I'm ashamed to say it but there's a part of me that doesn't want her to cross paths with the Hidden again now that they are hungry, now that they are hunting – just that very tiny little voice that had spoken the word *Stop* when I had Connie within sight of my arrow. Because she was so young, and so amusingly brave, and because none of this was her fault. Even though I was going to kill her.

Connie just sighs and pushes past me towards the door. I stand in her way and she turns back to face me, her face alight with anger. "You might have saved me back there in the woods, but you don't get to choose what I do now, OK?"

God take her eyes, why can't she just stay here? I let her go, swallowing the desire to slap her. Instead, I shoulder my bow and the quiver of arrows. I'm going to need every weapon I can carry. She stalks out of the door and away through the trees, golden hair shining all the way down her back, and it would be so easy to loose an arrow now, to watch her fall on her face like a felled tree. An arrow through the heart, through the lungs: she'd be dead before she hit the ground.

In the back of my mind, I still see the Swan King kneeling at my side when I fell from the tower at Fontevrault; I still hear the easy command in his voice when he told me to get up, those white feathers billowing around him, so pale against his black hair. He gave me a life worth living. Because of

Lissy, he's dead. *Patience*, I tell myself. *Let her die when Lissy can see her suffer.* Connie beckons me closer with an imploring look in her eyes, holding one finger to her lips. Connie has no idea how loud she is and here she is ordering me to be silent – I want to laugh.

I catch up, and Connie mouths at me, "*Listen.*"

And to my shame, she's heard something that I've missed. *Control yourself*, Larkspur would tell me. *You are not concentrating.* I stand still, forcing all thoughts of murder from my mind, and I listen. There it is – the sound of sobbing almost eclipsed by the thin, relentless wailing of a mortal child.

I catch up with Connie and she grabs my arm with her hand, her mortal touch so warm against my bare skin. "It sounds like a baby," she whispers. "Can you hear that?"

I'm here to hunt: I don't care. But Connie is already walking off towards the noise. A wailing child, a sobbing woman. This isn't going to be good. This is not something I need to be tangled up in, not now.

"Come back!" I hiss, but Connie ignores me. Damn Christ and all his angels, I should have killed her when I had the chance. She's running now, and I keep pace. Connie crashes through a tangle of briar, bracken and dog rose. I follow in silence. I hear the child quite clearly now, but the woman has fallen quiet – all I hear is unsteady breathing and now I'm closer I recognize the unhurried beat of a Hidden heart, always so much slower than the hot racing rhythm of a mortal's. I catch up to Connie and this time I hold her back; she flinches when I touch her, but she doesn't struggle.

Despite the Hidden mauling she endured last night she trusts me: more fool her.

"What?" Connie hisses. "Come on, that *is* a baby – we can't just leave it—"

"Wait." I hear myself say. "Let me go first – it's with the Hidden, and the Hidden don't have their own young." And once the Hidden have hold of a mortal child, they become desperate; they become dangerous. I've seen this before, too many times before the de Conways closed the Gateway. And slowly, steadily I step past Connie, treading in silence across last year's dead leaves. I weave my way through moss-covered oak trees, ash and thorn, and here in the green clearing before me is a wild young girl with ivy wound about the dark tangles of her hair, no girl at all but just Iris of the Raven Hair – Larkspur's lost love – and I haven't seen her for three hundred years.

Iris looks up, sensing my presence, her face glistening with tears as she tries to soothe the baby, rocking and rocking, but all to no good because mortal babies need to feed, and she is Hidden. She cannot feed it.

Her lips part in surprise when she sees me; she whispers my name. "*Nicolas*."

35

Larkspur

The air is thick with the sour scent of fear and desperation. As I move in silence through the panicking mortal teenagers, who haven't managed to find their way out of the woods, I notice older men and women pushing with brutal confidence amongst the straggles, dressed in the dark uniforms of mortal lawkeepers, circling ever closer around their target. Briar. It's Briar. Backing away from them.

I send an order: *Run, Briar.* At least I've found him.

And even as I wonder why Briar doesn't just turn and outrun these mortal lawkeepers as he so easily could, I hear his frightened voice in my mind. A single word: *Iron.*

I smell it now, too – like the hot scent of mortal blood, but far stronger, a punch of sickness to my stomach.

Larkspur—

Briar backs up against an ash tree as the lawkeepers step closer, one of them turning to reason with the throng of mortal girls behind.

"It's him!" one of the girls screams. "He did it! He attacked Tia Marshall and then Connie Harker, and now no one can find Connie!"

229

Briar's always been a fool but it looks like he's excelled himself this time.

Just stay still, I tell him. *Don't move.* Briar looks past the lawkeepers, never taking his eyes from my face: he trusts me to save his hide, the Swan King's son, and just as one of the female lawkeepers edges the crowd of girls away, I hear the clink of metal on metal, and Briar's eyes are stretched wide with fear. *Iron.* They have handcuffs. Steel handcuffs.

Don't move, I order. *Don't struggle.* If the cuffs break his skin, he'll die.

Just as I'm about to step forward and kill as many mortal lawkeepers as I have to, the air is rent with a high, wild screaming mingled with cries of astonished horror from the mortals. The rank stink of burning flesh fills the air, and as I watch, Briar disappears in a cloud of swirling, whirling dead leaves — he panicked, he struggled, and the steel cuffs must have grazed his skin, poisoning his blood with iron. The hot sharp stink of human spew fills the air as one of the lawkeepers crouches in the dirt, leaning forward, clawing the dirt as he vomits at the shock of it.

Briar has gone: I am too late, once again. Too late for my father, and now too late for Briar. Dead leaves whirl and drift and time seems to slow as if the air itself has thickened like stale milk, and even as I turn to walk away, useless now, I hear Lissy's voice in my mind, a loud, savage roar as if she were screaming right into my ear, even though she is nowhere near me.

Larkspur, Connie is with him. Connie is with Nicolas. Please help. Please help—

And I don't know if I should, because she killed him. She killed my father. Maybe it is time that Lissy suffered, too, and I ruin everything that I touch, anyway.

36

Connie

The Hidden girl cowered away from us, cradling the baby close to her chest. It was crying, but the cry sounded so thin and weak. And I'd have known that patchwork blanket anywhere: I spent three months knitting it. This Hidden creature had Amy's baby: she'd got little Mika.

"Stay back," Nicolas said, standing beside me. "Iris?"

Was that her name? It made her sound so innocent – a flower, a wild yellow flower that grows by streams and rivers, but she's a thief. A baby thief. *Mika.*

"That's not your baby." My heart pounded and for a second all I could hear was blood beating in my ears.

Iris backed away towards the trees, still rocking Mika from side to side, and all the time this thin, desperate wailing rang out through the trees. "My child," she whispered. Her face is wet with tears. "My little son."

Iris looked up, her eyes blurred with tears, and even though she was Hidden and I was mortal, her grief was sharp and clear. She was desperate. I shot a questioning glance at Nicolas, desperate to get Mika away from her, but I didn't have a clue how to get close enough and still make sure that

Mika didn't get hurt. He was so tiny, so fragile. I remembered the warm weight of his small body in my arms just the day or so before, no heavier than a cat.

"The Swan King took a mortal child captive – her name was Tippy," Nicolas spoke quietly. "Most of them died, but this one didn't. She suffered, though, just a little girl, desperate to go home, trapped in the Halls of the Hidden. Iris tried to release her and the Swan King found out. As punishment, he made her lie with a mortal knight and bear a hybrid child. The baby died because they usually do. Your sister and I are rare exceptions, and Iris never recovered. It must have been three hundred years ago at least, but the Hidden don't forget, Connie. Let me talk to her."

"Please don't let him die," Iris whispered, looking at me with pleading eyes. "Please don't take him away. I've waited so long to hold him again, and it feels a little better already, the hurting. But I don't know what to do. He won't stop crying."

"She's confused." Nicolas sounded surprisingly gentle. "She thinks it's her baby."

"He's not yours, that's why he's crying." I tried to keep my voice calm, patient. "He needs milk. He needs his real mother."

Iris looked down, crooning at Mika and stroking his dark hair, but still he cried and cried. "But I need my baby." Her voice broke like she was just some normal girl, so sad and desperate. "You don't understand. I need him. I couldn't help him. I just had to watch as the life drained out of him, and there was nothing I could do, and he was in such pain, and there was nothing I could do to comfort him." She wasn't talking about Mika any more, I realized, but that other baby, long ago – her baby – but to her, it wasn't long ago at all, and the grief was just as sharp and desperate as it had been on the day she'd lost her own child.

Nicolas stepped forward, very careful, arms at his sides, deliberately unthreatening. "Iris, the mortals won't let you keep this child. Briar attacked a mortal girl and now they're hunting us through the woods. They're afraid. Listen. The Hidden are free now – maybe one day you'll find another mortal to give you a baby – a bright-blooded mortal, and the baby won't die. It's not too late for that to happen, is it?"

Iris just cradled Mika, crooning and crooning. "It is too late," she whispered, gazing down at him with hungry desperation. "I know that, really. The mortals will come for me now, won't they? They'll punish me."

"It's not too late. Let me take him back," I said, trying to sound gentle even though every instinct was telling me to run at her and grab Mika. "I'll take him back home, and no one ever needs to know it was you who stole him. Go back to the Hidden – you'll be safe with them. Go back to Lissy."

I stepped towards Iris, but Nicolas grabbed my arm, and I sensed a terrifying and enormous strength: he wasn't going to let me get near her. I was slowly starting to realize that my assumption I'd been rescued by some kind of hero was a big mistake. Another one.

"You're not going anywhere. Bring Lissy. Ask her to come. *Find her:* you've done it before." There was something different about Nicolas's voice then. He sounded hard and cold, not like he was on the verge of laughing at me the whole time any more, but a lot like he was going to hurt me if I didn't do as he asked.

Iris backed away, rocking and crooning, rocking and crooning, and all the time Mika just wailed and wailed.

All I could hear was Iris, sobbing, begging, lost in the past again, trapped at the moment her child died three hundred years before. "Don't take my baby. I can't bear to lose him again. I can't bear it. Please don't take him, oh, don't take him, oh please don't—"

"Do it, Connie – call Lissy." Nicolas's voice was cold and alien, like he was a completely different person.

I needed Lissy, and I needed her now. I shut my eyes, trying to shut out Iris begging Nicolas to let her keep the baby. I reined in my fear and pictured my immortal sister again, her cloak of golden feathers, her wild red hair – so far away from the kind, quiet Lissy who had been just my big sister so long ago, never quite fitting in at school, always a bit different. Now she was a queen. Now she wasn't even human any more. I couldn't hear her voice in my mind, couldn't even summon a mental image of her that felt real. Wasn't I meant to be powerful; wasn't I meant to be Tainted? I was nothing – just a stupid little girl.

This time, nothing happened. Nothing at all.

37

Lissy

I soar high above the woods, wings spread, hunting for my sister. I saw her face in the water. She needs me. She needs me and I can't find her. Oh, Larkspur, I need your help. I need you now. *Forgive me, forgive me…*

38

Connie

Lissy's still my sister, I told myself, desperate, and instead of the wild queen I'd met in the woods, cloaked in feathers, I thought of Lissy as I really remembered her, my big sister curled up next to me on a huge double bed with a white duvet spread out all around us like fields of snow, reading me story after story. She never seemed to get bored of that. *Oh, Lissy—*

And just at that moment agonizing pain tore through my skull and my mind completely emptied like an upturned pan of water, leaving behind only the clear blue image of a wide open sky, blue and endless, punctuated only by the silhouette of not one bird soaring high above us, but two, wings spread, banking and swerving — a hawk and a falcon, hunting side by side.

Lissy—

"Damn it, they're coming!" I heard Nicolas cry out, and I opened my eyes to see the entire clearing whirling with feathers, brown, black and gold. Lissy and her brother Larkspur stepped out of the raging cloud of feathers, a furious red-haired queen and her brother, and then I was the one who was flying, so far from feeling like a failure and a screw-up that I wanted to shout with victory: I'd done this – I'd called them here with my mind, this wild creature Larkspur and this queen who had once been only my sister. *There's nothing I can't do now.* I'd done it after all.

39

Lissy

And through the storm of feathers, falling, tumbling feathers, I see the flash of Connie's golden hair, and stepping forward at my side is my brother, still at my side despite everything I've done.

"Larkspur—" He came. He answered my call.

And as the feathers clear, I notice Larkspur isn't looking at me, but at the dark-haired boy I met at sunset. The hybrid who will never die and he is holding on to Connie.

"*Nicolas!*" says my brother, and the ferocity of his tone is our father's – it is exactly as if the Swan King is here in the woods with us, and I find that I cannot move, that I cannot speak, that at exactly the point I need most to act, I am utterly frozen with fear.

40

Connie

Nicolas pulled me back so I was trapped, his arm pinning me back against his body, and I could feel his chest heaving with emotion as he dragged me round so we both faced Lissy. Iris sank to her knees, still cradling Mika, rubbing his back, whispering in his ear. The sound of his wailing was getting thinner and thinner, and Nicolas hadn't wanted to help me at all. He'd only wanted to hurt me. And just by my left ear, I heard a soft hissing sound and looked down to see the bright edge of a knife held against the side of my throat; I even felt the chill of it grazing my skin.

"Let her go," Lissy said. "Please—"

"Nicolas, my father is dead," Larkspur cut in. "Nothing can bring back the Swan King, not even this."

"I'll do anything," Lissy whispered. "I swear I'll do anything if you just let Connie go. None of this is her fault."

"You killed him!" Nicolas's voice rang out across the clearing, and as he shouted he held me tighter, and the knife quivered against my throat so that I could hardly breathe, and I felt a trickle of warm liquid running down my neck. "He's dead because of you." Nicolas drew in a deep, sobbing breath.

"I'm going to make you pay." He paused, his voice cracking with misery. "I'm going to make you pay for what you did, Lissy Harker."

The Swan King. He was talking about the Swan King, the boy from my Dream – the one Lissy had killed.

"Release her, or it will be you that pays." Lissy's voice was ice-cold as they faced each other.

Nicolas just laughed, and the blade of the knife flashed and glinted at the edge of my vision, and I knew my neck was bleeding. "There's nothing worse you can do to me now, Lissy."

I felt like the world was spinning too fast and I was caught in a strange stillness in the middle of it all.

"Nico," Larkspur said, gently now, "she's just a girl—"

Nicolas didn't move – the knife stayed. I could feel the chill of cold metal right against my throat, and God, how much was I going to bleed if he increased the pressure just a fraction more? Iris still didn't move; she just sat with Mika cradled in her lap, rocking backwards and forwards, staring at each of us in turn.

"I don't care. Lissy killed him!" Nicolas said, his breath warm in my hair. "She killed the Swan King. She deserves to suffer."

"Oh, let her go," Lissy sobbed, her face now wet with tears. "Just let her go, please. He wanted to die, Nicolas. I promise you he asked me to do it. He wanted it. *I didn't ask for this*. It wasn't my choice. Iris, tell them"

Iris looked up from cradling Mika. "My baby," she whispered, and despair washed over me. She wasn't going to help. All she cared about was Mika.

And then Larkspur spoke to her, very quietly in that hissing, rushing language I'd first heard in the wood less than twenty-four hours before. She looked up at him, watching his face. He dropped down to her level, making no sound, not even stirring a single dead leaf from the forest floor. And when he spoke again, it was easy to guess what he was really saying: *Please*.

Iris stared at Larkspur, her eyes lingering on his face for what seemed a very long time. And finally – finally – she turned to Nicolas and spoke in a rush, words crashing into each other, just tumbling out of her mouth. "I'm sorry. I'm so sorry. It's true. I showed Lissy the weapon, but the Swan King chose to die. Nicolas, you mustn't hurt the girl. It's not her fault. You had your freedom – the Hidden wanted theirs. Can you blame them? The Hidden *chose* me, Larkspur. Your father's time was done, and he knew the truth of it. I was the only one Lissy trusted – your father's own people chose me to find Lissy the right weapon." Iris shook her head. "She thought she could leave the Halls. She thought she could go home. We tricked her."

The silence continued for ever and ever, and for the longest time all I could hear was Nicolas breathing, ragged and desperate, until the cold chill of the knife against my neck fell away, and Nicolas shoved me out of his way. I ran to Lissy, who caught me in her arms, hugging me so close that I couldn't breathe. Holding my sister, I turned to Iris as she clung to the little blanket-wrapped bundle that was Mika, her face white and frozen with misery, her cheeks speckled with tears. The Hidden cried just like anyone else. Not so different after all. Nicolas dropped to his knees, head bowed, the knife lying abandoned among the tree roots.

"Thank you," I whispered, and I didn't even know which of them I was really talking to. These strange and beautiful murderous creatures.

Lissy just said my name over and over again, the feathers of her cloak brushing against my cheek as Nicolas bowed his head over the knife that would have killed me, the blade glinting in the early-morning light. In silence, Larkspur went and stood at Nicolas's side, laying one hand on his shoulder as he knelt in the mud and the dead leaves.

"Get up," he said, so gentle. "Can't you hear the mortals coming?"

"They want the baby, Iris," Lissy whispered, holding me even tighter, even closer to her body. "They'll kill you to get him back. Don't let them."

Nicolas got to his feet, and his face just looked hollow, and all that bright burning beauty just drained away. I couldn't help feeling sorry for him, despite the way he'd used me, despite the congealing trickle of blood on my neck. The woods were alive with noise – people shouting, leaves crunching underfoot, branches cracking, and all he said was, "We are running out of time."

I stepped away from Lissy, untangled myself from her embrace as I crouched in front of Iris. "I know what happened. I know what the Swan King did to you. But Mika isn't your baby. You remember what it's like to lose one, don't you? To never see him again?"

Iris just stared at me and I swear I could actually feel her longing, her desperate longing. And in silence, she held Mika up to me like an offering, like a sacred gift.

"Take him," she whispered. For a moment, her eyes lingered on Lissy, then finally on Larkspur. "I have done enough wrong."

I did the only thing I could do. I bundled Mika up as close to me as I could, his warm, tiny body in my arms, and I ran, leaving them all behind, zig-zagging through the trees. I couldn't trust any of them, not even Lissy: all I could do was run. I had to get Mika back to Hopesay Edge. I had to get him home to Amy, no matter how much it cost me, and no matter if I was blamed for taking him.

41

Joe

It was hot in the car even though it couldn't have been long past eleven in the morning. I couldn't call her: they'd taken my phone straight away, and Connie's was smashed in the woods. All I could do was sit in the back of the locked SUV parked up on the drive at the Reach, knowing the driver and her passenger were waiting inside for Connie. All I could do was just wait for it to happen. As I watched, a single police car pulled up beside the SUV. I caught sight of Connie's fair hair as the car door swung open and a policewoman climbed out.

They must still think I'm there to look after her. Waiting inside. The police would have made Connie call Dad and Miriam by now, but they were a day's travel away. I lifted my hand to bang on the window – anything to give her a warning, a few seconds' advantage, even just the tiniest chance of running – but the woman at my side just shook her head.

"Do you want her to get hurt? It's best if you don't interfere, Joe."

And all I could do was wait, a prisoner of the Fontevrault at last, trying to forget that one hundred years before, a boy younger than me had been shot for knowing too much about the Hidden. And now they had Connie.

42

Nicolas de Mercadier

Fontevrault Abbey, France

Sunlight pours through that window high in the tower where almost nine hundred years ago I crouched in bloodstained clothes. I remember the sweat in my hair dripping down my face and how loud my heart beat. The walls are naked stone now, those tapestries are long gone, long since crumbled to dust, just like my mother's bones, Anjou's bones and the earthly remains of all those who gathered here long ago to hold court with the Swan King: dust and worms. I feel as if I might have just stepped outside for a few moments and then stepped back in, except that so many centuries have passed – I am the knight in the old story who followed his lover into the fairy hill and stepped back out into daylight to find his mortal bones crumbling, except that for me, there is no escape into dust. No release from the world, no release from grief.

It's different at Fontevrault now. The room is bare save for the simple wooden table and chairs, never visited by the crowds of mortal tourists who spill through the courtyards and corridors where I grew up. It was so long ago, but if I shut my eyes and just listened I might easily mistake the crying child being dragged around the abbey by parents with cameras for one of the kitchen brats. I might easily imagine that I had only walked the earth for thirteen summers and had hardly ever left the confines of the abbey, always waiting for my mother to return with her glittering court, until one day she returned with a new husband, with Anjou, and I could tell straight away that he hated me. I can almost catch the scent of her – rosewater and hot lavender. But she is gone. They are all gone, so long ago.

Connie and her stepbrother sit apart, flanked on either side by men of the Fontevrault, separated by a Fontevrault woman who looks as if she might work in a bank – a crumpled grey suit, short, neat hair. The others gathered are no more noticeable – just the kind of men and women you might walk past in the street and ignore. The Fontevrault have changed just as the world has changed – descendants of those who sat here almost nine hundred years ago they may be, but there are no furs, no glinting jewels, no visible signs of exceptional wealth and power. And just as last time, I was not invited, but I still came, still I'm sitting at a table with them; I have evaded the Fontevrault for more than eight centuries. They will not take me now.

Gathered for only the second time in a thousand years, Hidden and Fontevrault together, we wait in silence as Connie stares at me across the table, still in the clothes that Briar tried to strip off her, days ago now. Her green eyes are cold and hard like river-bottom pebbles washed clean by the water: *You betrayed me.* And I wish I could tell her that I am sorry, but how do you begin to apologize for holding a knife to the throat of a fourteen-year-old mortal girl?

And even as Connie watches me, even as I absorb the hatred I know I deserve, the air fills with a million tumbling feathers, gold and tawny-brown, hawk-feathers, falcon-feathers. The faces of the gathered Fontevrault go slack with shock, and I realize most of them have never even laid eyes on one of the Hidden before – they have been driven underground for so long. No one really believes in fairy tales these days, not even the Fontevrault. But even though no one believes in fairy tales, when the feathers settle and wink out of existence, one by one, like stars blinking out of the sky at dawn, Larkspur and his sister, the Hawk Queen, are standing side by side in a room at Fontevrault Abbey, all the same.

Larkspur's eyes rest on me immediately. "I forbade you to come here." He is seriously angry, which always amuses me. "They would keep you prisoner till the end of time, Nicolas."

I shrug. "Do you really think I'd let them?"

Larkspur gives me a furious look, but turns to Lissy. She scans the face of the gathered Fontevrault as if there is someone here she expects to see, but does not. And when she speaks, her voice is that of a queen: "*Let them go!*"

The woman sitting between Connie and Joe just smiles. "I'm not sure why you think we're able to do that. Both of them have seen far too much of you, Lissy. Far more than those teenagers in the woods at Hopesay Reach—"

"Harm them and you will pay," Lissy interrupts. "If you kill my sister and Joe, or even if you only keep them as prisoners, the Hidden will keep appearing. You will never be able to catch us, not all of us. We will always be too fast, too secretive. We both know that the mortals of Hopesay Edge saw too much this time. Police officers. Hundreds of people up in the woods. Too much to write off. Too much for you to cover up if it happens again – people will talk. There'll be rumours and theories that even you cannot contain. Release my sister, release Joe, and I swear that the Hidden will remain out of sight until what happened at Hopesay becomes nothing but a rumour, just a story that no one really believes."

Joe glances sideways at Connie, but she doesn't move her eyes away from the table. Brave girl. "Do what you want to me, but leave her alone," Joe says, quietly. "Just leave it."

The Fontevrault woman only smiles again; the others simply watch, allowing her to lead.

"If you kill them, we will never go away," Larkspur says, quietly. "You might slaughter all the Hidden one by one, but till the last of us is dead we will appear to the mortals, we will seduce them, we will try again and again and eventually we will give them immortal babies till the race you feared might one day come into being walks the earth in their hundreds, just like my sister and Nicolas de Mercadier. We will punish you if you kill Connie and Joe."

And the whole of the world hangs waiting in the silence until the Fontevrault woman sitting between Connie and Joe speaks again: "Then go," she says, and turns back to Lissy and Larkspur. "We will always find them. If you don't keep to your side of the deal, don't forget that we will always find them. Don't let anyone see you, Lissy Harker."

Another bargain, another covenant, and I don't know who will break it first but we need to leave this place before the Fontevrault try. We made the mistake of staying too long in this place once before. It is time and more that we went.

43

Lissy

I hug Connie in the abbey car park, wrapping my arms around her as we stand by a black glossy hire car arranged for us by the Fontevrault. All the tourists have gone for the day, leaving only us – and them: the Fontevrault, watching us from the three nondescript SUVs parked by the entrance. Waiting to make sure I keep my promise. Larkspur and Nicolas are waiting for me, concealed in the shadow cast by the huge, looming wall of the ancient abbey. The feathers of my hawk-cloak pool in the dust at my feet. I can never walk in the open again, not if I'm going to keep my side of the bargain. Not if I want to keep the Hidden safe. It's so strange to think how none of those hundreds of tourists swarming through the abbey today ever knew how close they all came to dying, how much the Swan King wanted to obliterate them. It's over now. It's done. I glance over to the car park exit, to the SUVs parked like sleek black seals sunning themselves on a rock. The Fontevrault are ready. It's time.

"You should go," I whisper into Connie's ear. Her golden hair smells stale, unwashed. She and Joe could both do with a shower, a change of clothes, but at least the Fontevrault didn't hurt either of them once they were prisoners.

Connie pulls away, her face shining with tears. If we ever see each other again, it'll have to be a secret from the Fontevrault. And after the way they caught Joe and Connie at Hopesay, I'm not sure it's even *possible* to keep secrets from the Fontevrault. This might be the last time. The very last time I see my sister.

Connie pulls away, looking up into my face. "Don't do anything stupid, OK?" She glances at the hire car. It's dark, but I can see Joe sitting behind the steering wheel, leaning back against the seat. I think his eyes are closed. "Lissy," Connie goes on, quietly, "he waited a long time."

For me. "I know," I say.

I'm so conspicuous out here with my cloak of feathers. All it would take is a car full of French teenagers looking for a place to hang out, and the Fontevrault would end all hope of freedom for the Hidden. I can sense Larkspur's unease from here, even though he and Nicolas are waiting metres away, concealed in shadow.

Giving me a bright, brave smile, Connie opens the passenger side door, releasing a wave of vanilla-scented air-freshener, one of those smells from my past that reminds me with such horrible force of the time when I was just an ordinary mortal girl. Connie slides into her seat, ready to go. It's time to watch her leave, time to say goodbye. Joe starts the car, the engine hums, and I can't help myself. I run to his window, but he doesn't open it. He does look, though. He turns to look at me. When the Swan King first took me to live amongst the Hidden, Joe was the only one who tried to stop him. The only one who dared to believe that there had to be another way, even though there never was.

"Thank you," I say, mouthing the words through the darkened glass, knowing it can never be enough, that Joe lost so many years of his life to missing me, and there's nothing I can do to mend that but let him go.

Joe turns slightly, glancing at me through the window. He nods, as if in silent agreement, and all I can do is stand in my cloak of feathers, watching as the car pulls away. I was once mortal. I was once one of them.

Now I'm Hidden, and it's time to run.

44

Connie

Northern France, one day later

We drove north and the window on my side was filled with
glaring light as the sun went down, spreading pink and red
and yellow all over the sky, way too bright to look at, so I had
to look at Joe. He'd hardly said a word since we left the abbey,
since the Fontevrault let us go free. I tried to block out the
memories of the room I'd been kept in, those uncountable
hours, the terrifying overnight journey, bundled in and out
of unfamiliar cars, into a plane, and finally to the ancient
abbey where all this started, where Nicolas had grown up so
long ago. I pushed the hysterical phone call with Mum out
of my mind, or tried to. I wasn't ready to think about Mum
yet. I definitely wasn't ready to see her. So many lies. I stared
out of the window at the motorway flashing past. "No one'll
ever find out what really happened, will they?"

Joe just shrugged. "If the Fontevrault are good at one
thing, it's a cover-up. To be fair – how much will they have
to do if Lissy keeps to her word and the Hidden stay out
of the way? Who'd believe it?" At least there was nothing
they could do to my dad now, still lying cold and dead in a
hospital morgue. "It's over now. It doesn't matter any more,

Connie. We've just got to hope that the Hidden keep to their side of the deal, that's all."

He drew in a long breath, and I looked up to see that his face was wet with tears, and I knew they were all for Lissy.

"Where do you think they went?" I closed my eyes, partly because it was so awful to see Joe crying, and partly because I could picture Lissy that way much better. She seemed more real as I remembered her in our old life – just a mortal girl curled up at my side on the sofa, reading *Harry Potter* to me.

Joe just shrugged, and I knew he was thinking of the moment we'd been herded out of that cold stone room at Fontevrault Abbey, and how Lissy had been standing at Nicolas's side: two of a kind, the only two in all the world. I knew then that I would never be enough for Joe, always just a reminder of Lissy and what he could never have.

"Maybe it's not over." I forced out the words, anything to make it so that Joe wasn't driving me north, back to England, back to his grandad's till I was ready to face Mum, just driving along with tears streaming down his face. He'd always been there to pick up the pieces for me, for no other reason than it was the right thing to do. The least I could do was try and do the same for him. "I know Lissy's gone, Joe, that we can't see her again. But maybe that's not the end of everything. Why can't it be the beginning? You're free now. She doesn't own you any more. And she did, didn't she? Lissy really owned you for six whole years – she didn't mean to, but she did. Well, she doesn't any more."

Joe turned to me, half smiling. "Nice try, Con. It'll take more than that to fix me."

I raised both eyebrows. "Well, obviously. I *am* dealing with a screw-up of monumental proportions, after all."

And this time he really did smile.

"Listen, Joe. You didn't talk to Nicolas: I did. Lissy's just like him, and it's only going to be a blink of an eye for her before you and me are both old and then dead." I couldn't get my head around that at all, but I knew it was true, and I'd never forget the look on Nicolas's face when he talked about his family, all dead, all gone, their little lives just over so quickly, so insignificant compared to the Hidden. I couldn't sit there watching Joe get ready to watch the rest of the time he had slip past, dreaming about a girl he could never have, a girl who didn't really exist any more. Lissy was still Lissy, in a way. But she was also Hidden, and their queen. "We've got to make the most of it, OK? We're hardly here on earth at all compared with them. Don't waste your time, Joe. Promise me you won't waste it."

Joe leaned back in his seat, holding the steering wheel with just one hand. I could tell he didn't really believe he'd ever get over her. "I'll do my best, all right?"

I reached over and grabbed his hand, and he held mine, too. It was enough. "Promise?"

"I promise, Con."

"Good." And I let go of Joe's hand. Life's too short to waste on hope alone.

Epilogue

Larkspur

The Dancers, four years later

Iris and I sit apart from the others, watching the moon rise above the fells as we lean into each other. One of my tribe is singing the ancient songs of our people, songs of the rivers and mountains we left behind, of the dark halls we called home for so many centuries. The dancing has started, too, lean Hidden figures twisting in the moonlight by the old standing stones, free under the sky, but this time I feel no cause to dance and I'd rather watch, because Iris is with me, she has forgiven me, and that is enough.

"Do you hear that?" she says: the swift beat of mortal hearts. "They are coming."

This time there's no need to call our tribe to arms, to walk away into the sea, into the trees. There is laughter, too, a young mortal couple talking in low voices, laughing as they make their way up the hillside. I see them now, a mortal girl and a boy, hand in hand, silhouetted against the light of an almost-ripe moon.

They stop when they see us, and she smiles. "Hello, Larkspur."

I can't help smiling back. "You found us, then."

She shrugs. "It wasn't so hard."

And the boy is just looking on in wonder at the rest of my tribe dancing by the standing stones.

"How's Joe? Isn't he with you?" Has he forgotten Lissy at last?

Connie glances at Iris, then looks down the fellside at the tiny mortal dwelling nestled against the hill – a stone cottage with square windows lit up against the night. "Back at the smallholding with his girlfriend. They've got a baby, a new baby."

And Iris does not flinch, because now there is a life inside her that grows with every new moon. A miracle. A one-in-two-thousand-years' chance: worse even than the Fontevrault's worst nightmare. Not a hybrid child, but a Hidden child, and it's mine.

I smile, and I remember my father, what he once said: *On the day that you were born, and I held you red and bloodied in my hands, I knew such joy as I had never known.* And in the next breath he'd banished me, and that was the last time we spoke, and all I can do is hope that I don't make the same mistakes. "On and on, Connie Harker. On and on," I say, glancing at the mortal boy at her side, who is still staring in undisguised wonder at the dark, lithe figures dancing beneath the moon, twisting and spiralling around the standing stones. "What about your side of the bargain, Connie? Can he be trusted?"

She shrugs. "Yes. He saw, Larkspur. He was there in the woods that night. Lying only makes it all worse, doesn't it? Where's my sister?"

I watch Connie's face, hoping that she is right, and that

this mortal boy won't betray us to the Fontevrault. "She'll come."

And Connie turns to the boy at her side, still holding his hand. Two have broken away from the dancers, walking towards us both together. Lissy and Nicolas. "Look, Blue," she says, and the boy just watches with that same silent wonder written across his face, holding Connie close as she leans into his shoulder, waiting as Lissy and Nicolas cross the tangled moonlit grass. They're side by side, her cloak of feathers billowing out around her, wild hair tangled in the warm wind blowing in off the sea, Nicolas with his shirt loose around his neck, walking with a sense of freedom and ease that has only come to him lately.

And, laughing, Connie breaks away from the boy at her side, and she runs across the windblown grass towards her sister.

Acknowledgements

I am so very grateful to the tremendous Daisy Jellicoe, who never forgets a single plot detail, and also to Hannah Love, who will stop at nothing to make sure you love books as much as she does. Thanks are due of course to Catherine Clarke for her unending support, for which I'm always so grateful.

I am really indebted to the wonderful UKYA book bloggers who showed their support for *Hidden Among Us* and who spread the love for books with such passion. In particular I must single out Vivienne Dacosta, Sister Spooky, Clover, Hannah Mariska and Raimy Greenland, who all were kind enough to let me loose with guest posts on their blogs. Thank you so very much, guys.

I must also say another big thank you, this time to Mr Dart and Class 7Y1 at Ivybridge Community College in Devon, who brought my knowledge of school life up to the twenty-first century and explained the use of interactive whiteboards. I owe big, big thanks to a certain crew, last but never least, who shall of course remain nameless (Chatham House Rule, my dears).

BLOODLINE

IN THE WILD LANDSCAPE
of Dark Age Britain, Essa is abandoned by
his father in a lonely marsh-village trapped
between two warring kingdoms. Destined
to become tangled in the bitter feud, Essa's part in
it is more important than he ever dreamed. But how
will Essa save those he loves and discover the secret
of his true identity when he can trust no one?

*"A rich, vivid historical fantasy and a tremendously
assured first novel."* Philip Reeve

BLOODLINE RISING

CAI, THE GHOST, is the fastest, most cunning young criminal in Constantinople. A perfect life, until he is captured, bound and sent to Britain – the home his barbarian parents fled long ago. When he is taken in by Wulfhere, prince of Mercia, Cai soon discovers that his English master knows more about his family than he does. But war threatens and Cai finds he must choose: will he betray his new clan and save himself, or be loyal and risk his life?

"An excellent, well-written novel that makes a lasting impression." Books for Keeps

SPIRIT HUNTER

Two empires are at war.

This time, the Empress of China is sure she
will destroy the Horse Tribes for ever.

She sends a deadly weapon across the desert
with her army: Swiftarrow, her Shaolin spy.
But Swiftarrow has more than one mission to
complete. He must also find a new recruit for the
empress, a young barbarian to train as Shaolin:
swift as a shadow, more silent than death.

Out on the Steppe, a young Horse Tribe shaman
dreams of a great battle and the slaughter of
her people. She knows that war is coming.
She must stop the bloodshed. But how?

"Epic... Exciting..." Independent

Dangerous to know

Bethany + Jack

Two teenagers in love.

Why is everyone desperate to keep them apart?

"Beautifully observed." The Book Bag

Enjoyed this book? Tweet us your thoughts.

#HiddenPrincess @KatyjaMoran @WalkerBooksUK